MILES LEDOUX

KISS ME QUICK

Winter in Veil, Book 12

First edition

ISBN: 978-1-882508-92-1

Cover art by Rachel Kelli
Editing by Julie Mianecki

This book was professionally typeset on Reedsy.
Find out more at reedsy.com

Preface

All around the cobbler's bench
The monkey chased the weasel
The monkey thought 'twas all in fun
Pop! goes the weasel
I've no time to wait and sigh
I've no time to tease-l
Kiss me quick
I'm off
Goodbye...

Prologue

Nine-year-old Emma Thurmin had to choose her timing carefully.

"I just don't see how you could possibly be okay with us staying here!"

"Because I've thought it through and I know we'd end up coming back home *anyway,* regardless of whether things have changed."

Emma's parents had been arguing quite frequently the last few days. According to her classmates, so had a lot of other parents. The schoolteachers had been much stricter, too. Recess had been "suspended indefinitely," which made a lot of kids sad and angry. Everyone in town had been on edge since the serial killer had come back to Veil.

Except he wasn't "back," Emma's friend Kirsten kept reminding everyone. The killer couldn't be back because he'd never really been gone. The sheriff's department had arrested someone three months ago, and the killings had stopped, and everyone finally felt safe. But then, last week, Elijah Pressler, the mayor of Veil, had been shot to death, and the sheriff's department told everyone it was the serial killer who had done it. The man they'd arrested had to be released. Everyone started to live in fear again.

The voice of Emma's father echoed from above. "Sooner or later they're gonna call in the state police to help with the

1

investigation! By the time we finish packing, they'll have caught the guy!"

"Oh, like they caught him the last time?!"

"Well, what are we supposed to do?! Move out of Veil?"

"I'm not talking about moving, I'm talking about getting our family out of the town where the killer is!"

"If we were his next targets, he'd just follow us. We should stay on familiar ground."

"Oh my god, I can't believe what we're talking about…"

Emma decided the sliding door would be best; it had a carpeted floor just inside, and all the other doors were loud and squeaky. She'd already put her shoes on, since her boots would be noisy. The February weather was too cold for the snow to be slushy, and anyway Emma knew how to avoid deep snow. The bag of birdseed was already in her pocket.

"What if we just stayed with some friends for a few—"

"One of those friends could be the killer!!"

As her mother's voice reached a crescendo, Emma swiftly unlocked the door, slid it open, and stepped out of the den, into the snow.

Emma had discovered the robin's nest several days ago. Usually birds didn't lay their eggs till the spring, but at school she'd learned that climate change was causing birds to lay their eggs too early, and many of the babies were dying from lack of food and warmth. She'd been leaving birdseed in the hollow of a tree near the nest every other day. Robins' eggs could take two weeks to hatch, and she was determined to keep feeding the birds at least until then, though it was getting harder and harder to sneak out.

As she slipped into the shallow copse of trees behind her house, an encouraging sound met her ears. A chorus of tiny

2

chirps told her the eggs had finally hatched. How she wished she were tall enough to see into the nest! She'd better leave only part of the birdseed so she'd be able to leave more in a couple days. Hopefully her parents would decide to stay till then.

All her attention was on the birds' nest, so it wasn't until after she'd deposited the birdseed and turned around that she noticed the object sprawled on the ground.

She stopped short. Any thought of sneaking back into her house before her parents realized she was missing fled her mind as she gazed in horrified fascination.

Last October, Emma had had a most disturbing experience when she'd stumbled across what appeared to be a dead body. Even though it had later transpired that the woman was, in fact, alive, Emma could remember staring down at her and feeling sick…the glistening redness of the blood, the open mouth with seemingly no air passing through it, the stillness of the chest…

What she beheld now was lying on its side with its back to Emma. Not only was it completely still, it also seemed stiff. The angles of the limbs and neck felt somehow wrong. It was a woman, though much larger than the last one. Older, too. The skin was a very strange color.

Emma did something she hadn't been brave enough to do the first time: she stuck out her toe and prodded the body. It was too heavy for her to move. And then it struck her—when she'd found that other body, in her head she'd called her a "she," as if, deep down, she'd somehow known that it was still a person, still living. This…she could only think of as an "it."

Hurriedly she stuffed the rest of the birdseed into the tree hollow. She knew it would be a long time before she ever made it back.

I

"We are gathered here today to mourn the loss of a dear, beloved member of our community. A very special young woman...named Violet."

Over thirty years had passed since Jen Grogan heard those words, yet she remembered them clearly. It was the first funeral she had ever attended. Her father had come close to forbidding her from going, though if he had, she'd have gone anyway. Sixteen-year-old Violet Hall had been her best friend.

Until something terrible had happened to her.

She'd been murdered. And her killer was still in Veil.

Jen knew that now. Up until recently, it had only been a suspicion wriggling in the pit of her stomach, but finally—*finally*—she had confirmation.

In a few short hours, Jen would be attending another funeral, that of Mayor Elijah Pressler. By a quirk of fate, she, her daughter, and their close friend—coincidentally also named Violet—had been ear-witnesses to Pressler's violent demise. Jen hadn't heard all of it, as she had been racing to Pressler's home as fast as she could—arriving too late to save him—but Cyanne and Violet had heard enough to know that Pressler was the latest victim of Veil's serial killer, who it turned out was still at large. In fact, it seemed he'd been at large for a *very* long time.

4

"For such a promising young life to be cut short by a tragic accident..."

But Violet Hall's death hadn't been an accident. In her heart, Jen had always known that, had always said so, and now she finally had her proof.

At age eleven, Jen had found Violet Hall's body on an upper floor of a condemned apartment building. Violet had been bludgeoned to death. She had *not* fallen through a hole in the floor and plummeted several stories. That was what everyone else thought. Jen tried to tell the adults that there had been someone else in the building, that whoever it was had chased her till she'd fallen and passed out. If only she could show them where Violet had actually been killed, find some physical evidence to back up her story...but every time she tried to retrace her steps, it always led to a dead end. It was as if the inside of the building had rearranged itself. Or perhaps the killer had rearranged it...but that was a silly thought. (Wasn't it?)

Jen spent the rest of her adolescence faced with exasperated attitudes, for she refused to accept the lie of how her friend's life had ended. Some grown-ups patronizingly paid her compliments for her conviction, though from her point of view, it wasn't conviction at all, it was just a fact. She had *been* there. Her story was true and the official one was false. When, after graduating from high school, she'd announced her decision to pursue a career in law enforcement, her father had been furious. Perhaps he'd been secretly waiting for her to grow out of her silly fantasy, at which point she'd stop repeating her story and they could all forget it had ever existed. But devoting her life to the pursuit of justice was as good as shouting loud enough for everyone to hear: *You failed to get justice for my murdered friend.*

Jen had rarely spoken to her father since then. He probably had no idea that she was now the sheriff of Veil.

Now it was up to her to stop this serial killer once and for all. Moments before his death, Pressler had stated that the killer had been active at least as far back as Violet Hall's death—perhaps she'd been his very first victim. When Pressler asked the killer why he'd slaughtered all those people, the answer had come in a garbled, distorted voice: *"I made a promise."*

It was the same answer the killer had given Violet Grogan on that terrible night last November, when he'd called her and taunted her over the phone. That was the proof that it really was the same killer, and not a copycat.

The killer had taunted Jen that night, too, recreating the circumstances of the day she found Violet Hall's body. At the time, Jen had thought the perp was just trying to mess with her head, but now she knew—it really was the same killer! *Violet's* killer! Jen experienced a twinge of guilt at the joy she felt, the validation, her second chance to get justice for her friend.

That chance had come at a high cost. From all that Jen and her deputies could piece together, it seemed the killer had been active all over New England for three decades.

They could find no pattern to the killings, no indication of how he chose his victims or when or where he would strike next. Sometimes two killings might take place in the same weekend; other times there might be years before the next body dropped. The only connection between the deaths was that they all bore an obscure reference to a certain nursery rhyme.

Back in November, Deputy Benno had been the first to spot the clues deliberately left by the killer, alluding to the song, "Pop Goes the Weasel." The signs were so abstruse that at first Benno's theory had been ridiculed. Then two dead bodies were arranged in the backseat of his car, each with a name tag: "Monkey" and "Weasel." No doubt remained.

If the deputies' findings were correct, the frequency of homicides had increased over the last few years. Once the killings had reached Veil, more bodies had dropped than in any other town before it. *No,* thought Jen. Not "reached" Veil. *Returned* to Veil. Because this was where it had started in the first place.

"We commend her body to the Earth. Ashes to ashes. Dust to dust..."

Even after having known her for months, Jen still found herself amazed by Violet's incredible powers of memory. She wished she possessed some of those powers right now, as she scoured her own memory for recollections of the man who, until recently, everyone had been satisfied was Veil's serial killer. He would've been only a young man then, probably beardless and less burly. Jen hadn't officially met him till she'd moved back to Veil last summer, but if he was a lifelong Veil resident, it was likely she'd seen him at some point during her childhood. She tried and tried to picture him at her best friend's funeral, perhaps showing some sign of guilt she just hadn't noticed at the time...but all she could bring back were memories of her classmates—Amy Chester, smug for having even more ways to bully Jen; Myrna Redpath, the class oddball, surprising Jen by sticking up for her even though they weren't friends (Myrna was always ready to believe any story that was grim and ghastly).

No matter how Jen wracked her brain, she couldn't come up with a way to bring Kurt Riner back into custody. When they'd caught him last November, the evidence against him had seemed damning. If she weren't the sheriff, Jen wondered, would she have reported Pressler's dying words, knowing it would result in Riner's release? If only there were some hard evidence that the serial killer had an accomplice, they could hold him under suspicion. As it was, the idea of two serial killers working together was too much for the court to swallow. If there was still a killer out there, there must be one, and only one. So Kurt Riner had gone free, and the town was once again living in fear and dread.

And for that, the town blamed Jen and Violet Grogan.

No one had said it outright, but Jen could sense it: a look in people's eyes, a coolness in their manner, an unspoken resentment: *We thought it was over. You told us you caught him. We felt safe. We let our guard down because of you. You were supposed to protect us.*

You lied to us.

Violet had sworn up and down that Kurt Riner was the killer who'd terrorized the town that night in November, but it was no good. It didn't help her case when she had to admit that Riner couldn't have been the person who taunted her on the phone, not if that same person killed Pressler. Riner had been in custody when that murder took place.

The killer had told Violet that he and she had a "connection," but he wouldn't tell her what it was. Now Jen wondered: was that "connection" the fact that, over three decades ago, he'd murdered someone who bore the same name?

Was it *really* the same person? Could it really, *finally* be coming full circle? Just how old must this killer be?

A thought passed through her mind for the umpteenth time: *Maybe Riner killed Violet Hall, and since then he's groomed an accomplice.*

And for the umpteenth time, the same answer followed:
*Pressler accused **his murderer** of killing Violet.*

Jen and Violet Grogan had returned to the condemned building just the other day, not only to look for evidence against Riner, but also to try the impossible. Even after all this time, Jen felt she owed it to her childhood friend to locate the exact room in which she'd been killed. Without knowing where the murder had occurred, it felt to her as if the lie about her death still carried too much strength. As a traumatized child she'd had no success, but surely, as an adult, with the help of someone who had a perfect memory, she could finally decipher the puzzle.

Thirty years had done nothing to preserve a structure that was already deteriorating to begin with. Only a few recognizable landmarks remained, which amounted to a few partially intact staircases and half of what was once a full-length mirror leaning against the wall.

Jen thought of how she'd shone a flashlight on the mirror, illuminating two women staring back through the dirty glass. One was tall and lean, with pale blue eyes, a long, thin nose, and dirty blond hair pulled back in a pony tail. She wore a sheriff's badge and uniform. The other woman was much younger and shorter, with striking amber eyes and a purple streak in her dark hair.

Violet Grogan turned to Jen and said, "When you told us the story that night by the campfire, you mentioned seeing this mirror shortly before you found Violet Hall, and again shortly afterward."

"Yes," Jen murmured, almost to herself. "I saw my reflection, I crawled through a crack in the wall, I went through a door, and that's where I found Violet. Then I went back through the door, and I meant to crawl through the same crack, but I must have gone through the wrong one, because a few rooms later I looked over and saw this mirror again."

"How far away were you?"

Using her flashlight to navigate carefully around the holes in the floor, Jen traversed the hall to its far end, then looked back. Frowning, she took a few steps forward, then looked up again. "This far, I think."

"Did you see the mirror on your left or on your right?"

"My left." She turned left and found herself looking through a doorframe. She felt hope stir within her.

Violet made her way gingerly over to her. "Which way did you go next?"

"I…turned right." Jen pivoted such that her back was to the mirror. "I pushed my way through some debris, and then I found a staircase, but I couldn't go down 'cause the steps had caved in." They went over to the nearby stairwell.

The steps were intact.

Jen deflated. She felt Violet's reassuring hand on her shoulder. "Why don't we try backtracking from the mirror instead?" the younger woman suggested.

They tried. And tried again. Despite Violet's willingness to help, Jen found herself resenting her, and felt ashamed for it. But after all, why couldn't *she* remember things perfectly? What good was it to someone who hadn't witnessed her best friend's murder? Jen was the one who needed the ability now. Without it, she was nothing but a failure.

Jen was startled out of her reverie when the phone on her desk blared to life. She blinked through her disorientation, remembering where she was: her office in the sheriff's station. She cleared her throat and picked up the phone. "Sheriff Grogan."

As she listened, she slowly straightened in her chair, her color draining. She gave curt instructions, then hung up and allowed herself one deep, heavy breath before she stood up and set off to do her job.

* * *

Cyanne Grogan had an older sister, Azura, who had been in Antarctica for several months as part of an internship. Cy knew her mother frequently worried about Azura in such a harsh environment, but she had a hunch that, if it were possible, her mother would send Cy there, too, and force her to stay until the serial killer was caught. The next best option was one that many Veil families had exercised: no child was allowed to be alone at any time. At this moment, Cy was with her next-door neighbors, helping them pack.

One of those neighbors was a classmate of Cy's. Two of their other classmates were also there. It might have felt like a party if not for the awful circumstances. Cy caught a glimpse of herself in a dresser mirror, and saw a tear trickling down her cheek. Quickly she brushed it away, pretending to fidget with her chestnut brown hair. Sad though she was about her friend moving away, right now she wanted to be supportive, not a burden.

"There's a good daycare, at least," Kristy Dosley said thickly as she nursed a seven-month-old baby girl.

"You've been to the town before?" asked Cy.

Kristy nodded, sniffling. "We stay there whenever we visit my mom's family in the Hudson Valley. Fran wanted to move there right after, um, what happened last fall. Mom talked her into staying." She broke down into quiet sobs.

Stationed at Kristy's bedroom closet, where she was helping her friend pack up her clothes, Cy was about to go over and comfort her, but she was beaten to it by one of the other two helpers.

Feeling a hand on her shoulder, Kristy looked up into Em West's eyes. She squeezed their hand and held it for a minute as she wept.

Then Kristy whispered, "Rosie's asleep. I'm going to put her down for her nap." As she carried the baby out of her bedroom and into the nursery, Em's eyes followed her. A certain expression flickered there for a moment, then was gone—but Cy had seen it.

After laying the sleeping Rosie in her crib, Kristy turned around to find Cy standing there. "Do it now," said Cy.

"What?"

"Tell Em how you feel about them. This could be your last chance."

Kristy led Cy into the hall and closed the nursery door. "I can't tell them now!" she whispered.

"Why not?"

Deflating, Kristy made a helpless gesture. "What's the point if I'm moving away?"

"Yeah, I know," Cy agreed, "the timing sucks. Everything that's going on right now sucks. But no matter what you do, it's not going to suck any more than it already does."

"Don't say that," Kristy pleaded in an ominous voice.

"What I'm trying to say is that you can't possibly make things worse—"

"Oh my god!"

"By telling them what you've been working up the courage to tell them! And you'll regret it if you don't!" After a moment's hesitation, she added, "Believe me."

Cy and Kristy returned to Kristy's room together, but Cy deliberately entered first and asked, "Neesha, could you come help me with something?"

"Sure," said Neesha Davis.

Cy waited till Neesha had come out and Kristy had gone in before shutting the door firmly. "Walk loudly," Cy whispered.

"What?"

"Walk loudly, so they know we're going away."

Bemused, Neesha complied.

Cy brought her to the end of the hall overlooking the stairs, and suggested they wait there a minute. They waited so quietly that Joy and Fran, Kristy's parents, didn't notice them as they passed by on the floor below.

"Did you finish packing the glassware?" Fran asked.

Joy didn't respond. She kept walking, as if Fran didn't exist. Fran stared after her a minute, then heaved a sigh of bottled emotion and headed off in the other direction.

Cy knew that, despite being Kristy's parents, Joy and Fran were not a romantic couple, but it still broke her heart to see one of them giving the other the cold shoulder. This year had been so unfairly hard on them. They deserved better.

Cy and Neesha waited a few more minutes before tip-toeing back to Kristy's room. Cy carefully eased the door open a crack, and she and Neesha peeked through.

Em and Kristy had their arms around each other in a quiet, intimate embrace. Cy couldn't see Kristy's face, but Em was planting soft, tender kisses just below her jawline. Kristy pulled her head back and looked into Em's eyes. With their thumb, Em brushed a tear from Kristy's cheek.

Normally, when Kristy was happy, the whole world soon knew about it. This time, Kristy's happiness seemed so profound, she was moved to silence. As she beamed at Em, they glanced down shyly, but they were smiling, too. Kristy grasped the side of their head and kissed them gently, tenderly.

A cooing sigh escaped their throat.

After silently shutting the door, Cy and Neesha both mouthed an exuberant *Yes!!* and hugged each other.

* * *

Violet brushed sweaty hair from her face, then leaned down to kiss her lover.

Candy's breath caught and she shut her eyes in pleasure and amazement. Soft cries of ecstasy escaped her lips.

After a while, Violet gasped and crawled slowly forward, kissing her way along. Candy's body still quivered underneath her. When Violet reached Candy's mouth, she kissed her hungrily, as if trying to steal her breath. She pressed her skin against Candy's, twined her fingers in hers, moved with her in a pulsing rhythm.

Candy still had her eyes shut, but eventually she opened them wide in astonishment. She reached up and caressed Violet's face. Violet's eyes opened, too.

What she saw in them made Candy go instantly still. "What's wrong?"

With a guilty look, Violet rolled sideways, and Candy propped herself up on an elbow. "Violet, what is it?"

Violet was still catching her breath, but the look in her eyes expressed a feeling too deep to be put into words.

"Hey." Candy clasped the side of her neck. "It's okay. Whatever it is, I'm here for you."

Violet's eyes dropped. "That's just it. I...want you to go."

"You what?"

"I want you to leave Veil. Don't come back till it's safe."

Slowly Candy shook her head. "I'm not gonna leave you."

"I need you to."

Candy raised a semi-stern eyebrow. "Would you leave me?"

Violet flashed a conciliatory smile, then worry replaced it again. "The last time it felt like this here in Veil, when the killer left me that phone and messed with my head…" She forced herself to keep looking into Candy's eyes. "That was the day I kissed Trisha. And that night he took her. She almost died." She swallowed. "If anything happened to you…"

Candy reached over and kissed Violet on the mouth. It was a different sort of kiss, one that had a message: *I understand. Don't be afraid. It'll be all right.*

After the kiss, Candy spoke aloud: "Come away with me."

An aching look came into Violet's eyes…then she shook her head. "I can't. I have to stay and help stop him. It's my fault he's been at large these last few months."

"That's not on you."

"I convinced everyone that Kurt Riner was the serial killer. I still think he's involved—in fact, I *know* he is—but it never even occurred to me there might be a second killer. Not until I heard Pressler…" She shivered.

"And Pressler didn't leave behind any clue as to who killed him?"

"Jen and the deputies went through his files thoroughly. There was barely anything on his computer. Benno thinks Pressler had some sort of dead-man switch so that if he died, like, maybe there was a code that if you don't enter it every so often, everything incriminating gets deleted. Either that or someone erased it for him."

Candy said with quiet anguish, "It might be a long time before you catch the killer."

"I'm sorry," Violet whispered.

For several seconds they gazed at each other, heedless of the chill spreading over their naked bodies as they lay together on

Violet's bed. Finally, Candy heaved a deep sigh and slid her hand over Violet's hip to her lower back. "You figured out who was stalking me," she said. "You can solve the mystery of who's stalking Veil. And when you do, I'll be waiting."

Slow smiles spread across both their faces. "You better be," said Violet.

Gently Candy rolled Violet onto her back and straddled her, becoming a human blanket. After a minute, she repeated Violet's actions from earlier, though in reverse, kissing her all over while crawling backwards.

For a blissful hour, the serial killer and the rest of Veil didn't exist.

* * *

Sheriff Grogan approached the tree with the hollow full of birdseed. She'd left Emma and her parents in a neighbor's house across the street. A voice in the back of her head was shouting, *Who is it? Who did he get this time? Who?!*

The last time Emma Thurmin had come across such a discovery, it turned out to be not a corpse but the live body of a woman with amnesia, who everyone knew today as Violet Grogan. Of course, it had taken some time for this discovery to come to light, for by the time the sheriff responded to Emma's parents' nine-one-one call, Violet had come to and wandered off. Where Emma had found a "corpse," there was no body to be seen, alive or dead.

Sheriff Grogan turned a full three hundred sixty degrees.

There was no body here.

"No," she murmured, shaking her head emphatically. "No, no, no, no, no, no…"

II

"We're gathered here to pay our respects, and to remember a man who was a pillar of the Veil community: Mayor Elijah William Pressler."

Was it Violet's imagination, or did the same expression flit across the faces of all the people assembled in the churchyard? As if, for an instant, the same thought flashed through everyone's minds: that in fact no one was, at this moment, thinking about Mayor Pressler. In his place was an ubiquitous unspoken certainty...

The serial killer is probably here right now. I might be looking at him. Or her. Or them.

As the preacher's voice droned on, Violet, wearing black and sitting between Cy and Candy, let her gaze drift over the assemblage.

Sixty-something Hal Clayton looked out of place in a suit. Violet was used to seeing the tall, shaggy man in wool and flannel. For a man his age, he was quite spry and limber. Prior to Jen Grogan's relocation to Veil last summer, Hal had been the senior deputy in the Veil sheriff's department. He had been good friends with the previous sheriff, Keith Dubowski; perhaps he'd also been close with Dubowski's buddy, Kurt Riner. Hal had a reputation for having courted friendships all over New

England. Had his visits to those towns coincided with any unsolved homicides?

Violet thought back to her first meeting with Hal, remembered how friendly and helpful he'd been since then. With iron resolve, she squashed down her rising guilt. The stakes were too high to rule *anyone* out, no matter how kind or otherwise unlikely they seemed. This killer, whoever he was, must seem unlikely, or else he'd have stood out long before now.

She tried to keep this in mind as she turned her gaze toward Rabbi Isaac Metz.

Back in October, on the night Violet and Candy had first kissed, several people had attended a Wiccan sabbat at Candy's mother's house. Among the attendees were Rabbi Metz, whom Violet had met a few days prior and liked very much...and a young man named Matt Foley, who, it was now believed, fell victim to the serial killer the very next morning.

Metz and Foley had arrived for the sabbat at almost the same time. Although neither was aware of it, Violet had witnessed their arrival from inside the house, through a window. All the attendees were required to undergo "smudging" before joining the ceremony (a simple process involving handheld incense and a large feather). Matt Foley, an adamant—some might even say militant—atheist, had refused the protocol of spiritual cleansing so belligerently that it nearly escalated into a case of trespassing right then and there. Rabbi Metz had resolved the altercation by offering to take over the smudging duty from the young woman Foley was arguing with. Metz did not have a threatening nature, yet Foley seemed far less confident about defying the rabbi than he had about disrespecting a woman (Candy had diagnosed it as simple misogyny).

At the time, Violet had been relieved and grateful for the

rabbi's intervention. Now, knowing what had happened to Foley just a few hours later, she couldn't help but fixate on the last words she'd heard Metz speak to the doomed man as he wafted incense about his body:

"If you don't mind, I'll start with your back."

The coroner's report indicated that the first of the many blows that crushed Matt Foley's body had struck him on his back.

It *had* to be a coincidence…didn't it?

The rabbi's eyes suddenly flicked toward Violet, who blinked and pretended to be looking somewhere else.

Her eyes landed on Chuck Benz, the *Veil Chronicle*'s newest reporter. Chuck had had a narrow escape three months ago, when a booby-trap left by the serial killer nearly made him another murder victim. At the last minute, Violet had remembered a crucial detail, giving Deputy Benno a chance to save Chuck just in time.

Thus Chuck Benz was the only person in Veil—apart from the Grogans—whom the serial killer had targeted and had survived.

Was it possible the attempt on his life had been staged? Was it a ruse to clear Chuck of suspicion? Could *he* be the serial killer? She'd gone over events in her head many times, trying to see if there was a way Chuck could have faked his brush with death. Perhaps if he'd been monitoring the sheriff department's communications, he might have heard that Benno was heading to the building where the booby-trap was set, and got there ahead of him. He'd have to have timed it *just* right…

For a moment, Violet felt certain she'd landed upon the solution. Then she reproached herself. The fact that a scenario in which Chuck turned out to be the villain felt more *comfortable* to her did not excuse her attaching more credence to that possibility than to others. Not that she had anything in particular against Chuck, she simply didn't place him among those she was closest to.

Then again, Chuck Benz had shown a lot of deference to Kurt Riner before Violet named him the serial killer. Could Chuck be Riner's secret accomplice?

The only other person Violet had seen act friendly toward Riner—apart from Amy Chester, who, until her untimely death, had been Riner's fiancée—was Kelly Upshaw, former *Chronicle* reporter. Kelly had been Amy's aunt, and, following her niece's death, had been convinced Violet was involved in her murder. Kelly had even gone so far as to abduct Violet, to try to force a confession out of her. No matter what, Kelly refused to believe Riner was responsible for Amy's death.

Could all of that have been an act? Was Kelly actually Riner's accomplice? Violet doubted it. In any case, Kelly had left Veil soon after that incident. No one had heard from her since. Her trial was due to begin next month.

"And now," said the preacher, spreading his arms wide, "I invite those of you who have stories and memories to share to step up one at a time and give them voice."

Mayor Pressler might not have been universally liked, but Violet was sure there were a few in Veil who would want to talk about him. However, no one seemed to have the courage to go first. Violet looked inquiringly at Cy, who shook her head firmly. Violet understood: Cy still needed time to sort out her feelings about Pressler before she ever thought about sharing them.

Finally, someone rose to his feet and strode to the pulpit. When he passed by Violet, she felt a deep shiver. It might have been the cold, or perhaps it was the fact that Deputy James Derrick had grown his new beard exactly in the style of the late Sheriff Dubowski. Despite the posthumous revelation that Jen Grogan's predecessor had been an attempted rapist and would-be murderer, Derrick's idolatry for the deceased sheriff clearly remained alive and well.

Violet could remember vividly the bearded face, the powerful hands choking the life out of her…

"Good afternoon, everyone," Derrick said solemnly. "I'm Jim Derrick, senior deputy with the Veil sheriff's department."

Cy and Violet exchanged sharp glances. As far as they knew, Cy's mother had not yet chosen a deputy to promote to her right-hand position.

"Sheriff Grogan intended to be here," Derrick went on, "but she was called away at the last minute."

An uneasy murmur passed through the crowd. Had the killer struck again? Had another victim been found? Or victims?

Derrick seemed to sense the mood of unrest he'd inspired. "I know all of you are scared. And I know it feels like we let you down."

Violet felt a twinge of guilt and winced.

"Even if we didn't see eye to eye, Mayor Pressler was one of our citizens. And, I admit, if we hadn't pegged the wrong man as the serial killer, maybe he'd still be alive."

Violet heard sharp gasps on either side of her, but she was too stunned to make a sound. She stared up at Deputy Derrick in outrage and indignation.

"But we're on the case now," Derrick promised, not looking in Violet's direction. "And I swear to you we won't rest until the real killer is behind bars. You can count on us to keep you safe." His eyes darted once in Violet's direction as he finished, "We won't let you down a second time. Thank you."

As Derrick returned to his seat, the preacher moved toward

the pulpit. Before he could say anything, someone else marched up and took a stance behind the microphone. Mutters and whispers abounded—even some grumblings of disapproval. Violet couldn't blame them. She wasn't sure what she was about to say, but she knew in her heart she had to say *something*.

She took a deep breath. "We…we all…" She cleared her throat, tugged the microphone down closer to her mouth. *Whatever I say, I should at least say it like I mean it,* she thought to herself.

She looked out at the crowd and spoke clearly, steadily. "I want to share something about Mayor Pressler. Something I'll always remember, regardless of my history with him. Pressler and I… We weren't friends. Not at all. But just before he died, he did something for me. I was listening when it happened. The person who took his life also threatened my life. And Pressler…"

"I know who Violet really is! After all this time, I've finally found out! She is the last *person you want to cross! She's really—"*

BANG!

Violet's breath caught for a moment, then she regained her composure. "Pressler tried to save me by lying, by tricking the killer. He didn't have to do that. To be honest, I don't know why he did. But if he were here, I'd thank him."

The preacher moved forward with anxious eagerness, but Violet wasn't done. "And I would promise him… I *promise*…" She gave the crowd a hard look as she laid stress on the word. "I'll find whoever did this to him. And they will pay."

Her gaze slid casually across Deputy Derrick on her way back to her seat, and she caught him glowering at her. She didn't respond.

When she reached her chair, she paused for a second, then she seemed to change her mind about sitting down. She grasped

Cy's and Candy's hands and whispered, "I'll see you guys later," before strolling straight out of the churchyard.

She met up with Jen Grogan around the corner, out of sight of the funeral-goers. "I'm glad you saw me waving from all the way over there," said the sheriff. "I didn't want to cause a panic by interrupting the service and taking you away."

"What's happened?"

"I need you to look at something, see if you spot anything that I can't."

"Is it a crime scene?"

"I—don't know. Whatever it is, it's not good."

* * *

With Violet having left, Cy and Candy kept each other company after the service was over. Together they sat on the church steps and watched their fellow funeral-goers disperse.

"Everyone's so quiet," Cy observed, "even for a funeral. They're all looking at each other but trying to hide it."

Candy noticed a few openly suspicious stares directed at her. "Not all of them," she muttered.

"Hey, I just realized... Is your mom okay?"

Candy sighed. "We're still working through our issues. I wanted to stay with her, but if Violet's right, I might be putting Mom in danger. She's already told me she's not leaving Veil. I talked her into staying with some friends. What about you?"

"What do you mean?"

"Well...does your dad know what's going on here?"

A hard look came over Cy. "I don't know. If he does, he hasn't said or done anything." She shook her head in growing exasperation. "I'm sick of having these complicated feelings about all these stupid guys—Dad, Pressler, Rob... I just wanna be done with guys until this is all over."

Among the departing funeral-goers was a teenage boy who glanced over, saw Cy, and did a double-take.

She saw him and her breath caught. It was Luther Hennessey, whom she'd dated until he left her for another girl. As far as Cy knew, he was still dating her.

Luther, not having taken his eyes off Cy, walked straight into a parked van.

Cy stifled her laughter. Then she blushed.

Candy, pretending not to have noticed this exchange, said under her breath, "Famous last words."

* * *

Emma carefully folded the paper so that the edges aligned. Printer paper was more difficult for someone with small fingers to fold into origami, but she went about it slowly, with intense patience and focus.

Emma's parents had taken her to the neighbor's house across the street to wait for the sheriff. They'd waited together in the living room, watching their house through the front window, until Emma had gotten bored. She was allowed to wait in the study, where she'd been given permission to use the printer paper for drawing. Emma thought they wouldn't mind if she used it for a different kind of art. She'd made two cranes, a fish, and a pattern she'd made up on her own which might be a turtle or a beetle.

She could hear the sheriff talking to her parents now. Soon the sheriff would want to talk to her, just like last time—only then, the sheriff had been a man. To her surprise, when the study door opened, it wasn't the sheriff or one of her deputies. It was the Memory Girl, whose name was Violet.

"Hi, Emma," Violet said with a smile. She was pretty, and she seemed friendly.

Acutely, Emma said, "You didn't find the body, did you. It's gone."

Violet looked uncomfortable. "Um, I think your mom wanted to be the one to… No, we didn't find her. We looked for clues but didn't find any."

After a moment, Emma went back to her origami endeavor.

Violet sat next to her at the desk. "But we did find a lot of birdseed out there. Somebody's been making sure those birds have enough food."

Emma's latest creation was looking more birdlike with every fold.

"Do you like birds, Emma?"

"Mostly I like unicorns, but birds are my favorite non-magical animal."

"Were you feeding the birds when you found the woman?"

Emma paused, glanced at the open door, then lowered her voice to a whisper: "I've been sneaking out every day to feed them."

Violet whispered back, "I think your parents have already figured that out."

"Oh." Emma sighed. Then she asked, though she already knew what the answer would probably be, "If the lady isn't there anymore, does that mean she's alive and she got up and went away—like you did?"

Violet's face became like a rock. "I don't know," she finally said in a voice that was slightly singsong.

Emma went on conversationally, "At first I thought it was you again. You were the first dead body I ever saw."

Violet chuckled. "Yeah, I remember."

Emma blinked. "You remember?"

"Yeah, I saw you when you found me."

"If you saw me, why didn't you say anything?"

"Well, I wanted to, but…I was too tired."

Emma thought for a minute, then said, "I'm sorry I ran away and didn't help you."

"Oh! Hey." Violet gently touched Emma's shoulder. "Don't even worry about it! I'm all right."

Echoes of shouting voices reached them. Emma wrinkled her nose. "They're fighting again. They're not gonna stop until Dad gives in and we leave Veil."

"W-well…" Violet looked uncomfortable again. "Maybe going somewhere safer for a while wouldn't be a bad idea."

"Because of the serial killer?"

Violet nodded slowly. "Yes."

"What about you? Are you leaving?"

"No, I'm staying. I'm helping the sheriff."

"You're gonna catch the killer?"

Violet gave a dry chuckle and opened her mouth to answer. Then she paused. An air of resolution came over her. She looked directly at Emma and said in a serious voice, "Yes. I am. I'm going to catch him."

"Before he gets anyone else?"

Another pause. Violet's expression didn't change. "Yes," she said. "I promise. We won't let him kill any more people."

Something in her voice made Emma believe her.

* * *

Violet reported what she'd learned to Jen as they drove back to the church.

"So that's it," Jen said grimly. "The killer knew how to stage the body being discovered and then vanishing—just like you when you first appeared in Veil—because Emma was sneaking out to the tree every day." When she saw the troubled look on

Violet's face, she added, "He's trying to mess with you again. He knows you're a threat to him and he's trying to throw you off your game."

"It's not that…"

"What is it?"

Violet squinted, as if to make her puzzled thoughts become clearer. "I don't know. It feels like…we're missing something."

They picked up Cy and Candy and filled them in as they drove back to the Grogan house.

Cy immediately turned to Violet with trepidation. "Who wasn't at the funeral?"

Violet had already been compiling a list in her head. "A lot of people," she answered gravely.

"But I mean—anyone we know?"

Violet hesitated, then said to Jen, "You might want to check on Myrna and make sure she's okay."

"Who's Myrna?" asked Candy.

"Mom's weird friend," said Cy, hastily adding, "but she's cool."

"We'll start checking in after I release the information to the radio station, and they can report what's happened," said Jen. "I have to avoid starting a panic if I can."

Instead of pulling into the garage, Jen parked in front of the house and led the three young women to the front door. "Just change your clothes and come back," she instructed. "We'll head straight to the station. Candy, we'll drop you off on the way." She unlocked the door and opened it.

The very first thing Violet saw was Roswell, the Grogans' calico cat, batting at shoelaces where the outdoor footwear was stored on plastic mats. Then, in the next half-second, as the door opened the rest of the way, she saw what was lying just inside.

Candy gasped. Cy screamed. Jen started shouting orders and pushed them all away.

The missing dead body had been found.

III

"You're listening to KVLM. This is Rod Piper with the local news. It is with great regret that I report the death of Kelly Upshaw, former reporter for the Veil Chronicle. She was found one hour ago by Sheriff Jen Grogan. Full details of Ms. Upshaw's death have not yet been released, as the investigation has just begun, but it has been confirmed that the cause of her death was homicide. For more, I have Sheriff Grogan here with me in the studio. Sheriff?"

"Thank you, Rod. As you said, I can't give a full report on Ms. Upshaw's demise while the investigation is still ongoing, but we have reason to believe she's the latest discovered victim of the Veil serial killer, who has been terrorizing our town since October. I'm giving out this information now because I know many people already suspect it and it's leading to a town-wide panic. Just on the way here, I observed a traffic jam on Main Street because of people trying to leave town. Everyone, please don't panic. If you decide to leave, do so calmly and carefully. There's no sense in getting yourself injured while trying to flee from danger.

"Look, I know this is scary. I know it feels like we're in a horror movie. I do urge you all to be vigilant, but please remember you're still part of a community. We have to find ways to work together in spite of all this. If you're worried about trusting a person, well, then *trust two more. Or five more. Separating and isolating ourselves from each other makes us easier targets, not harder ones.*

"My deputies and I are going to get to the bottom of this. We'll keep you apprised."

"Thank you, sheriff. We'll be on standby here at the radio station, ready to relay any important updates."

* * *

Violet stood beside the staircase in the Grogans' front hall, regarding the body of Kelly Upshaw. The coroner had finished her examination. The only reason the body had not yet been taken away was so that Violet could have a chance to look it over, to see if it triggered anything in her memory.

Violet was wearing a loose-fitting outfit, which Kristy Dosley had let her borrow so she could change out of her funeral attire. She, Cy, and Candy had been sent to wait at the Dosleys' while the investigation got underway. As soon as it was deemed safe, Violet had been allowed to look over the rest of the house to see if anything had been tampered with. As far as she could tell, nothing had been touched. The only items that had changed position were tiny objects one would expect a cat like Roswell to bat and jostle. Evidently the intruder had merely broken in through the front door, dumped the body, and left, locking the door behind him.

For it was plain that Kelly Upshaw had been killed somewhere else and then brought here. Her form was rigid, positioned deliberately so that it would be seen by those who entered. The body had become a prop in someone's show, in two acts. The first act had been staged for Emma Thurmin—who, a few minutes ago, had identified Kelly Upshaw as the body she'd found when shown a photograph from the *Chronicle*—and this was the second act.

30

The likelihood of the killer having left any valuable clues on Kelly's person was extremely low, but Violet gave it close scrutiny anyway. The most conspicuous feature was the set of bruises on the woman's large neck. Had she been strangled? Her eyes were closed, and her body didn't show any sign of paroxysm. Perhaps she'd been drugged first. Violet reflected that, in order to strangle a woman of Kelly's size, drugging her beforehand would practically be prerequisite.

She also reflected on how coolly these macabre thoughts passed through her head, and she shuddered a little.

The jacket was the same one Kelly had been wearing the last time Violet had seen her. One of the pockets had been torn open. Violet made a mental note to keep an eye out for a nail or some other protrusion somewhere in Veil with a thread of a matching dark blue color—until she spotted the culprit, a splinter of wood sticking out from the corner of the bottom step. No lead there.

Perhaps that was the reason Kelly's body had been left here. The killer wanted to shove a message in their faces: *I can kill anyone I want and you won't find a single clue.*

Anyone I want...

Why had he chosen Kelly? Violet had wondered plenty of times what made the killer decide to target the victims he had, for there seemed to be no pattern to it. The killings had occurred in dozens of towns across New England over many years; only within the last few months had they been limited to one town in particular. Whatever goal the killer was after— the "promise" he'd alluded to—Violet had a hunch they were entering the endgame. This close to his goal, the killer would want to dissuade Violet from getting in his way, so what better method than to leave a corpse in her own home? Except—

once more, Violet tried not to be distracted by her seeming cold-bloodedness—except, again, why choose Kelly Upshaw for such a purpose? Finding her body had been horrifying, traumatizing even, but…well, Violet had never much *liked* Kelly. A better choice for the killer's purpose would've been someone Violet was closer to.

Mentally she shut her eyes against sudden unbidden images.

Was it possible that the killer's purpose was something else altogether? That really it had nothing to *do* with Violet? Perhaps the body had been left here as a distraction. Perhaps, if the body had been found in another place—or at another *time*—it would have given away something about the killer's motive or identity.

"Do we know how long she's been dead?" Violet asked a deputy just then coming down the stairs. "Or can we not tell because the body was frozen or something?" She heard a sigh that was partially a groan. She looked up.

The deputy she'd spoken to was Deputy Derrick. He regarded her with annoyance—and something else which she couldn't identify, some feeling he was repressing too well to show. "Why are you here?" he drawled.

A few other deputies were nearby, finishing processing the crime scene. They paused in what they were doing.

Violet, who had been bending over the body, straightened up and stood squarely before Derrick. "Excuse me?"

"What are you here for? I'm not asking rhetorically," he snapped when she didn't answer right away.

"I don't think you're asking anything at all," she returned. "I think you're trying to *say* something, and you're trying to use me to make a point."

Derrick drew back his lips in growing ire. "You're here to *tell us things,*" he snarled. *"We're* the investigators. You give *us* information, not the other way around." He started to turn away.

The sharpness in Violet's voice stopped him. "What exactly is your problem, Deputy? Or, excuse me—*Senior* Deputy?"

He turned back to her with frightening calm. "Don't you ever talk to me like that," he said in a quiet, dangerous voice.

Derrick had always been less than sociable since she'd known him, but he'd never treated Violet like this before. She stood her ground. "This is not disrespect," she said. "This is someone calling you out for inappropriate behavior."

"Inappropriate—!" He sputtered in outrage. "You want to talk about inappropriate behavior? Let's talk about you discussing our cases with the public."

"I didn't mention the investigation. I only talked about my personal experience—"

"I'm not talking about the mayor's funeral!" Derrick shouted. "You've been telling people that Kurt Riner is the serial killer!"

Violet was taken aback. "You bet I have! He's dangerous, and he's been set loose! I have to warn people! He's welcome to sue me for slander. I'll gladly go to jail if it means protecting—"

"It's not your *job* to protect people! That's my—that's *our* job. Stop looking at me like that!"

Violet was giving him a very quizzical side-eye.

Derrick pivoted and opened the front door. "If you can't show respect for law enforcement, then you should leave the premises."

Violet almost laughed. "This is where I live."

"STOP CONTRADICTING ME!!!"

Perhaps it was the beard that so resembled that of the most recent person who'd tried to kill her, but as Derrick advanced on her, Violet had a sudden flare of panic, a deep-felt certainty that her life was in danger. She felt the wall slam into her behind before she even realized she was backing away in fright.

All at once there was a third person between her and Derrick. Deputy Benno was calm, but his eyes flashed warningly.

Shaking his head and fuming, Derrick stormed out the front door.

Violet fought to quit shaking. She felt Benno's gentle hand on her shoulder. "Thanks," she managed to say.

In a low voice, Benno told her, "Kurt Riner knows we have our eye on him. He's not going to risk getting caught again so soon after being released."

Violet swallowed. "He could still—do something."

"Then we'll do what we're trained to do—follow the evidence. Eventually we'll find something that ties him to the murders, or to the other killer."

"Then we need to hurry."

"Hey!" came Derrick's voice from outside. "Where do you think you're going?"

A softer voice answered, "I'm just—"

"You can't go in there yet!"

Violet bolted out the door, followed by Benno.

Candy was halfway up the path to the porch. "I told you," Derrick snarled at her, "you have to wait for the coroner to take the body before you can go back in!"

"I'm just here to say goodbye to Violet," Candy explained as Violet came to her side and took her by the arm. "My dad's on his way to pick me up."

"It's okay," Violet assured her.

"No, it's *not* okay!" Derrick's voice snapped out like a whip, causing Violet to shriek. He thrust his finger in her face. "You don't say whether or not—"

"Derrick!" Again Benno interposed himself, arm outstretched, fingers spread. "Stand down!"

Derrick blinked. His spine straightened so that he seemed to grow taller. In a low, threatening voice he asked, "What did you say?"

"Stand down," Benno repeated. Violet couldn't believe his calm.

Derrick eyed him weirdly. "Are you giving me orders?"

For the next few seconds, no one moved a muscle, which made the tension twice as thick. Neither man seemed willing to break it.

"May I!"

Both men did a double take. "What?" said Derrick.

Violet spoke clearly, pacifyingly. "May I say goodbye to my girlfriend?"

In turn, Derrick gave each of them the stink-eye, lingering last and longest on Benno before huffing and muttering, "You want to be in charge of this? Go ahead." He stomped off to his patrol car and drove away noisily.

As Benno headed back up the porch steps, Violet caught up to him. "Are you okay? For a second, I thought he was going to—"

"He wasn't," Benno reassured her.

Violet didn't look reassured.

As Candy joined them, Benno said, "I'll give you two some privacy," and went back inside.

Violet looked at Candy and saw her worry reflected in her lover's expression. She pulled Candy to her and held her as tight as she could, drinking in her scent, listening to the beat of her heart.

"Call me," Candy said faintly.

"Every day."

They kissed. Despite her dread, Violet promised herself it wouldn't be the last time.

At the end of the kiss, Candy hugged Violet once more. When they pulled apart, Candy was staring over Violet's shoulder. Violet turned. The front door was open, Kelly Upshaw's corpse on display.

Violet said, "It's weird, considering what Kelly did, but I feel kind of sorry for her."

"Yeah, me, too." After a moment, Candy took Violet's hand and looked at her inquiringly. When Violet nodded, Candy closed her eyes and inhaled deeply through her nose. "Mother Goddess, Father God, we release ourselves from those who have left this plane. May they walk the blessed gardens of eternal summer. Earth, Sun and Moon, give us life, death, and rest, and guide us through the night. Blessed be."

* * *

Candy's father drove her out of Veil by a back road in order to avoid the gridlock still jamming the Main Street intersection. Sheriff Grogan had sent Deputy Trent to direct the traffic, but there wasn't much he could do to ease its flow. He stood in the center of the intersection, little fearing he might be hit, for his seven-foot-tall frame was hard for drivers to miss (visually speaking). For hours he pointed his long, aching arms right and left, directing traffic this way and that. Out of the corner of his eye, he registered some activity in the nearby park square, the center of Veil, but he focused his attention on the drivers, keeping an eye out for the ones who were more panicked than the rest.

It was well into the afternoon before Trent was able to step onto the sidewalk and watch the cars pass smoothly beneath the traffic lights. There were no more long lines of waiting traffic; those who had chosen to leave Veil had all gone. One could only guess how many—or how few—were left.

Trent needed a moment to rest his legs before he reported in. He sat on one of the benches in the square. As the ache in his calves began to subside, he took greater notice of the small crowd gathered in the corner of the park. He squinted, then, a moment later, did a double take. Activating his radio, he said, "Deputy Trent calling Sheriff Grogan. Over."

"This is Grogan. Go ahead, Trent."

"Sheriff, traffic's back to normal, but I just thought you should know, Myrna Redpath is here in the park square."

"If she's pitching a tent, don't worry about it."

"She's selling knives."

"Are they switchblades?"

"No. They look homemade."

"They are. Is she selling to kids?"

"No, most of her customers are women about her age, late fifties."

"Myrna's forty-two, same age as me."

"Oh. Sorry."

"Give her a friendly reminder to card her younger-looking buyers, then I want you back at the—" A swell of static cut her off.

"Sheriff, please repeat, I didn't catch that."

But a new voice sounded over the radio: *"This is Deputy Ziegler at Twelve Meadow Drive, requesting backup! Possible hostage situation! Do you copy?!"*

* * *

"Stay inside," ordered Deputy Tan.

Mrs. DePalma obeyed, shutting the sliding door and backing away from the glass.

37

Behind the DePalmas' large house, a man's figure was crouched by the circular swimming pool. Tan and Ziegler crept toward him. From a closer distance, they could see that the man was aiming a rifle across the wide backyard. His target appeared to be a small, barn-shaped shed.

"Mr. DePalma," Ziegler said with carefully measured calm, "we're from the sheriff's department. I need you to—"

"He's there!" DePalma's eyes were fixed on the shed. "I've got him pinned!"

"Mr. DePalma, I need you to set the rifle slowly on the ground."

DePalma gave the deputies a fleeting glance. "Did you hear me?! It's the killer back there!"

"I hear you. I promise, he's not getting away. But I need you to put the rifle down."

The butt of the rifle shook in the man's hand, belying the calm in his voice. "He's on my property. I'm not disarming till my family's safe."

Ziegler threw an uncertain glance at Tan, who stepped past him and spoke. "Sir. We're on your side. But we will disarm you, ourselves, if we have to."

For several breaths no one moved. Then, without taking his eyes off the shed, DePalma handed the rifle over. Ziegler unloaded it and told the man to return to the house.

"I'm waiting here," DePalma said stubbornly.

Tan and Ziegler each made a wide circle, approaching the shed from either side. When they were level with the shed's front door, Ziegler called, "Veil Sheriff's Department! Identify yourself!"

A tenor voice answered, "Uh...I'm, I'm Luther! Luther Hennessey! I live just over there!"

Ziegler couldn't see him from where he was, but he imagined Luther was pointing in the direction of his house. "Luther, are you armed?"

"Um…" A thick, clublike tree branch flew out from behind the shed and into the woods. "No?"

"Luther," called Tan, "why are you on the DePalmas' property?"

"I'm—I'm looking for my dog! He got loose and ran this way."

Ziegler came a few steps closer. "Luther, are you sure you're not carrying a firearm? If you are, you're not in trouble, but you need to tell us now."

"No, I, I don't have a gun!" Luther sounded bemused.

Tan closed in from the other side. "Luther, the neighbor who flagged us down heard you threatening Mr. DePalma."

"What?!"

"She heard you telling him you were going to shoot him in the leg."

"What—no! That's what *he* said to *me!* He told me to stick my leg out from behind this shed so he could shoot me, or else he's gonna kill me!"

Tan and Ziegler took another step at the same time, and each saw a scared-looking—and empty-handed—Luther backed against the rear wall of the shed.

"COME OUT OF THERE!!"

Mr. DePalma took the deputies completely by surprise as he approached holding a *second* rifle.

Ziegler took a quick step and lifted a hand, fingers spread. "Mr. DePalma, stand down! Put the rifle on the ground and go back to your house!"

DePalma ignored him. "Come out from behind there, right now! This is your last warning!"

"Mr. DePalma!" shouted Tan. "It's not the killer! It's just a kid! He's not armed!"

"Mr. DePalma, it's me!" called Luther. "I didn't mean to be a trespasser, I was just trying to get my dog back!"

DePalma shook his head very slowly, his eyes hardly blinking. His breath sounded strange. It took the deputies a moment to realize he was whispering, muttering the same words again and again: "It's not going to be us next. It's not going to be us…"

"Sir," said Ziegler, "I know you're scared. I promise you, Luther is no threat."

"It's not going to be us. It is *not* going to be *us*."

"Look, I'll come out, okay? Just please don't shoot me—"

"Luther, *do not move!*" ordered Tan.

Ziegler took another, slower step. "Mr. DePalma, I am giving you *your* last warning. If you hurt anyone here, *you will be breaking the law.*" When this got no response, he went on, rather exasperated. "Just think how stupid and tragic it would be if any of us hurt each other—when *we're all on the same side!*"

DePalma licked his lips and swallowed. He whispered something the deputies didn't catch.

"What was that?" Ziegler asked hopefully.

More audibly DePalma whispered, "He makes an excuse. That's what he does."

With a sickly expression, Ziegler reached for his sidearm.

"He makes an excuse—and we let our guard down. Once… Twice… He comes onto our property, and we do nothing. There's a maniac coming into people's homes and killing them, and we know it—but when we have the chance to stop it, we do nothing. I let him go now…it's the same as letting everyone in…*everyone—*"

"Mr. DePalma, get down on the ground now." Ziegler's pistol

was out and held in DePalma's direction, though it was still pointed downward.

Finally DePalma spoke directly to him. "I haven't broken any law. You have no legal right to detain me."

"I'd rather get suspended than let you shoot an innocent kid."

DePalma trembled with rage. "I'm allowed to shoot *anyone* if it keeps my family safe!"

"You're *really not.*"

DePalma turned his head slowly toward Ziegler.

Tan saw the look in DePalma's eye. "Luther, GET DOWN!!!"

What would have happened next would forever remain uncertain, for Luther's lost dog chose that moment to make an abrupt appearance.

Startled by the furry object speeding by in his periphery, DePalma pivoted and fired.

He didn't hit the dog, for Deputy Tan was standing in the way.

IV

For a moment Benno was thrown by the sight of Deputy Derrick sitting behind the desk in the sheriff's office. He relaxed a little when he saw that Derrick was just using her phone.

"Yeah, I'll get that started," said Derrick. "Right." He hung up the phone.

"Was that the sheriff?"

"Yeah." Derrick came out from behind the desk.

"How's Debbie?"

"Who?"

"Deputy Tan, how is she?"

"She got lucky. Bullet went straight through her leg. She has to stay in the hospital, but the doctors say she's gonna be fine." Derrick headed for the door.

Benno blew out a heavy breath of relief. A moment later he shook his head and murmured, "Why didn't Ziegler wait for the sheriff before engaging?" He rubbed his eyes and took some deep breaths. When he felt calmer, he answered his own question: "Things must have gone south fast. He handled it as best he could."

A soft breath behind him made him turn, and he jumped to see that Derrick had not left the room. Derrick stood on the threshold with his hand on the door, looking at Benno in an unsettling manner. Closing the door, Derrick said, "You really think that's the reason?"

"What? What do you mean?"

Derrick took a step toward him. "Don't pretend you haven't noticed. Especially when you're part of it."

"Excuse me?"

"Ever since Grogan did her little morality test on the deputies, they've all been hiding their resentment—you included. You might follow her orders, but your loyalty to her is gone, now that you know she had to *test* your integrity before she believed in it."

Benno almost preferred the Derrick who had gone alpha-male on him earlier to this version that was apparently trying to engage in psychological jousting. "What are you saying, that it's Tan's fault she got shot?"

"Why would it be Tan's fault? She's not the leader. She's not responsible for how well her team works together."

Benno looked away and shook his head, dumbfounded.

"I know you've been thinking these things, too, Benno."

Benno almost smiled in spite of himself. "You know what I think? I think you're an opportunist. I think you don't give a damn about the cohesiveness of our team. You're trying to sow dissent. You're calling yourself the 'senior' deputy. You're doing everything you can to make yourself out to be the real leader of the department." Something occurred to him. "Is that why you helped the sheriff with the sting? So you could turn us against her afterward?"

It was strangely comforting to see the return of Derrick's trademark pout. "At least I'm not making excuses for her, defending her when she doesn't deserve it."

"*You* defended her once. Remember? When Rob Mulroy's body was discovered, and she was a suspect?" When Derrick had no ready response, Benno went on, "And let's not forget the number of times you defended and sucked up to Dubowski."

Derrick was incensed. "And you're not sucking up to Grogan? Following her lead in spite of her betrayal?"

Benno had opened the door to leave. Now shutting it firmly, he replied, "No. I'm not. I do what I do, and I do it to the best of my ability, not because I'm blindly loyal to someone, like you are, but because it's my job."

Derrick stepped almost nose to nose with him. "So if she ordered you to do something you thought was wrong, you wouldn't do it?"

Benno opened his mouth to respond...and found himself not saying anything.

"Yeah. That's what I thought," Derrick said, and left.

* * *

Luther Hennessey looked so dazed, he seemed not to notice when someone sat next to him on the bench in the sheriff's station hallway.

"Hi."

Luther looked over and found Cy sitting with a meter of space between them. Her expression was tentative. "Hi," he replied dully.

"I heard what happened. With Mr. DePalma." When Luther didn't respond, she added, "Mom put him in the jail just now."

At first it seemed Luther wasn't listening. Then he spoke in almost a whisper: "He was gonna kill me." He looked at Cy, then at the floor. "I don't think he really even thought I was the serial killer, but he was still gonna..."

Cy nodded sympathetically. "That's horrible."

"The weird thing is, part of me is kind of impressed by him. He was willing to do anything to protect his family." He rubbed his eyes and sighed. "I don't know. I don't know what I'm saying. Maybe I should've left Veil, too."

"Do your parents not want to leave?"

"What? Oh, no, they *did* leave."

Cy's jaw dropped. "They left you behind?!"

"Well, I kind of told them I wanted to stay, and we kind of fought about it."

There was a pause, then— "THEY LEFT YOU BEHIND?!! Your own parents??!"

"Well, foster parents."

"That's still messed up!!"

Luther gave a half-shrug. "I'm not too bummed about it. They're not my real family."

Cy shook her head, at a loss. After a moment, she gave up trying to make sense of it. "So why did you want to stay, then?" Before Luther could answer, she uttered a quick "Oh" of comprehension and looked down, reddening. "Because of Laurie."

"Nah, Laurie and I broke up. I wanted to stay 'cause I was just finally getting my grades back up. I don't want to fall behind and have to catch up all over again. That'd suck. What about you? Why are you still here?"

Cy gave a sigh. "We talked about it, me and Mom and Violet. Tried to figure out which is less dangerous, staying here where there's a psycho killer, or sending me away when we know Kurt Riner's out there somewhere. I fought him, you know, last November. The night Amy Chester and Byron Temple got murdered. And not to brag, but I totally saved Mom and Violet from Riner. Like, I kicked serious ass. And Riner, he fell through a hole in the roof of a condemned building. I still want to know how he survived." She paused, then said, "What I'm trying to say, underneath my rambling, is that the bottom line is…all three of us, we feel safer when we're together."

"When you're with family."

"Yeah. And at least, being together, we don't worry about each other as much as if we were apart." Her bottom lip trembled, belying her words.

Luther took her hand.

A second later, he let it go and gasped. "I'm sorry, I shouldn't have done that! I just—but you—I'm sorry." He looked away and palmed the top of his head.

Cy said quietly, "I don't mind."

* * *

On one wall of the sheriff's station bullpen was a large map of Veil. Despite being somewhat dated, it was still fairly accurate, at least as far as street names and locations. When Sheriff Grogan encountered the rarity of a whole minute uninterrupted, she stepped over to the person staring at the map, seemingly entranced. "You okay, Violet?"

Violet gave her a momentary glance. Her eyes were hard with concentration. "In my head, I'm going over everything that's happened in Veil since we last saw Kelly Upshaw alive. There's got to be a reason the killer preserved her body, a reason he didn't let her be found where he killed her. If he had, it would've given us a clue. I know it's a long shot."

"I have no problem with long shots," murmured Grogan, "especially as we don't have any leads."

One of the deputies called to her, and she moved off, leaving Violet shifting her eyes from one spot on the map to another, imagining Kelly's body being found in each location, and what it would mean if it had…and felt a mounting frustration. For she had already gone through the whole of Veil; nowhere held significance. She refused to believe the killer's decision had been arbitrary, but she couldn't see any alternative. Not unless dumping the body at the Grogans' had a purpose that hadn't played out yet. With a swell of impatience, Violet wished she could remember the future rather than the past.

She sank into a nearby chair and covered her face.

Pondering where the body had been found had gotten her nowhere. She was back to the question: *why* Kelly? Why *any* of them? Well, then again, for two of the victims, at least, there was an answer. Mayor Pressler had apparently stumbled onto the killer's identity, which ultimately had resulted in his death and that of Rob Mulroy, an intern with the local paper and Cy's ex. Who did that leave?

The faces of the Veil victims were posted on a bulletin board behind her; Violet could see them in her mind: Matt Foley, Marcy Temple, Jen's friend Violet Hall, Chuck Benz (almost), Amy Chester, Byron Temple, and now Kelly Upshaw. And a lot of people in a lot of other towns in the intervening years, throughout New England and even a few beyond.

Someone had wanted these people dead. *These* people. But what connected them? Nothing the deputies could find, except that, for most of them, the murder methods all made obscure references to one of many verses in the song, "Pop Goes the Weasel."

The killer wanted it known that the deaths were connected, but didn't mind if it took a very long time for the connection to be seen—which it had.

"Sheriff?" called Deputy Ziegler. "There's been an accident."

"Where?"

"Just out of town, almost in Platte. Semi and a Jeep. No one's hurt, but both parties are blaming the other."

"Go take statements. Make sure they both have transportation if they're not planning to stay in Veil." When at first Ziegler didn't move, she added, "We'll let you know if there's any change with Debbie."

Ziegler started for the door with a sigh of aggravation he took no trouble to conceal.

Grogan spoke sharply. "What was that, Deputy?"

Ziegler stopped in his tracks, and after a few tense moments, he responded tightly, "Nothing, ma'am."

After he'd left, Cy approached her mother. "Is everything okay?"

Grogan shook her head. "I'm gonna have to call in the state police. This is just more than we can handle. Between panicked drivers and what happened to Tan, it's only a matter of time before there's a fatality, killer or no killer. Things are getting out of control." It was at this point that she noticed Luther, who had followed Cy into the bullpen. She pointed at him and said sternly, "That does not get repeated."

"Oh—no, ma'am." Luther shook his head earnestly. Then, apparently deciding it would be wisest to keep talking, he said, "Glad no one was hurt in that accident. My neighbor got killed driving a semi last year, Mr....uh...ah...Mr.—" He pointed. "That guy's uncle."

Benno, seated at one of the computers and reading the preliminary report from the coroner, happened to glance over when Luther spoke and saw where the boy was pointing. At first, he merely turned back to the computer screen...

Then, as Cy and Luther were leaving, Benno called to them sharply, *"Wait!"*

Violet turned, startled, as did everyone else, and watched as Benno rapidly crossed the room.

He came straight up to Luther. "Whose uncle?"

"Huh?"

"Whose uncle died in an accident last year?"

"Oh. His." Luther tapped a photo on the serial killer bulletin board.

"Foley... What was his name?"

"M-matt Foley. You just said it."

"Not him, his uncle! The man driving the semi! What was his name?"

"Oh, um, Paul, I think."

"Paul Hammond," said Deputy Derrick. "I remember that."

Benno's lips moved, mouthing the name several times, as his eyes darted to several points across the bulletin board.

The energy in the room was changing. Violet could feel it. She exchanged glances with Cy.

Benno took a step back, almost dazed, with a look of dawning comprehension. He turned from the board to the sheriff. His eyes shone with the light of an epiphany.

"Benno, what is it?" said Grogan.

Benno licked his dry lips. "What if the serial killer—or killers—didn't leave their signature at every one of their crime scenes? What if there were even more victims—victims we don't know about?" He gestured to the board. "We didn't even know some of these *were* murders until we made the 'Pop Goes the Weasel' connection."

"Why would the killers do that?"

"Because the song *is not a signature at all.* It's a distraction! Something that keeps us from seeing what *really* connects the victims!"

"What connects them?" breathed Violet—though she, too, was beginning to see glimmers of clarity.

Benno tore a sheet of paper off a notepad, scrawled a large *PH*, and pinned it to the bulletin board next to Matt Foley's photo. "Paul Hammond—dead in an accident," he said, "and later that same year, his nephew is dead, too."

Violet drew a slow gasp. She pulled out her phone and started writing a text to Candy.

"You think Hammond was a victim of the serial killer?" asked Grogan.

Derrick gave a snort of derision.

Benno ignored him and said, "Sheriff, look at the pattern. Byron and Marcy Temple"—he pointed at each photo in turn—"father and daughter. Amy Chester was Kelly Upshaw's niece. Every other town where the murderer struck before Veil, whenever he claimed more than one victim, they were always killed simultaneously—*and they were always related.* Husband and wife, two sisters, mother and son, father and son—"

"Benno," Grogan interrupted, "I'm desperate for a breakthrough, but most people around here are related, distantly or otherwise. What you're describing sounds more like coincidence than a pattern."

Violet's phone dinged, signaling she'd received a response to her text. Quickly she read Candy's answer to the question she'd asked. "Jen!!"

"What?"

"Matt Foley and Marcy Temple were first cousins."

For a full three seconds, all was silent and still.

Then the sheriff began barking out orders, and within minutes, everyone was on the phone or their email, interrogating people across the region, within law enforcement and without.

While she waited for results, Sheriff Grogan took over dispatch duty, coordinating with the deputies who were still out on patrol.

Derrick was the first one to uncover something. "Sheriff! The victim in Stowe and the victim in Brattleboro were half-siblings. Same father, different mothers, but as far as anyone knows, the siblings never actually met. They were twenty-five years apart in age. They were killed within two months of each other."

Benno had hung up and was copying down what Derrick reported. Then he added his own: "The victim in Springfield and the ones who died on interstate ninety-one—the sisters— they weren't directly related to each other, but they shared a cousin—a first cousin, from different sides of the family—who died *in between* them, chronologically, down in Florida."

"Murdered?" asked Grogan.

"Ruled as accidental suicide."

"Accidental suicide…" The sheriff looked as if she were having an epiphany of her own. "Benno…that woman who died of exposure last month, Sharon Brisbon…"

"Yeah?" Benno sounded encouraging.

"We couldn't find anyone who could tell us about her personal life. In the end, she turned out to be Amy Chester's great aunt, but we only found that out by accident—because Amy wasn't alive to tell us about her."

"Right…?"

"What if Amy wasn't the only person who wasn't alive to tell us something?"

Benno caught on quickly. "I'll check up on Byron Temple's genealogy."

"Mom!" Cy hurried up to her. "Mom, Chuck Benz is also Paul Hammond's nephew. Like, a great-great-nephew."

"Who told you that?"

"Chuck." Cy held up her cell phone.

"Tell him to get over here."

"Okay."

The next few minutes saw the accumulation of more and more information. The bulletin board became inundated with names and relationships, deepening the scope of the tragedy while adding to the promise of revelation.

At one point Violet caught sight of Jen Grogan staring off and shaking her head. She could just make out her whispered words: "How did we miss this? How could we…?"

Violet felt moved to tell her that Candy was the only one who knew of the blood tie between Matt and Marcy, and she'd left town before they were murdered. If Sheriff Dubowski had neglected to seek out and interview Candy, then that was on him—

But before Violet could speak, Benno slammed down the phone in triumph. "Sharon Brisbon was Byron Temple's aunt! That makes him Amy's first cousin once removed and Kelly's… um…"

A voice interrupted. "Sheriff…"

Violet was startled by how shocked Deputy Derrick looked. Anything extraordinary he encountered he tended to treat with skepticism, incredulity. She couldn't recall ever seeing him so stunned. He was having trouble hanging up the phone.

"What is it, Derrick?"

Derrick nodded at the phone. "That was the sheriff in Frost, New York. He said it was a coincidence, me calling up and asking about the woman killed there four years ago…because earlier today someone else called and asked for help finding that woman."

"Who was it?" demanded the sheriff.

Again Derrick gave an uncharacteristically dramatic pause. "It was a lawyer. A probate lawyer. The sheriff said he asked why the lawyer was looking for the dead woman. The lawyer told him it's because the woman is the heir to a fortune. The *Lammwych* fortune."

V

I t had been almost two months since a lawyer had appeared to Violet out of the blue and made the bizarre accusation that she'd laid claim to the vast fortune left by millionaire Torrance Lammwych, a town legend. At the time, it was thought that Torrance's adopted daughter, Roberta, was an heir to the fortune, but as she had been missing for many years, the money had been frozen in an account for all that time. Seeking to clear her name, Violet had investigated and uncovered the truth, that the actual heir was Torrance's son, Bobby, whom everyone had mistakenly assumed had been disinherited. Since Bobby was no longer alive, it had fallen to the lawyers to determine who was next in line to inherit.

The fact that those lawyers had landed upon one of the previous murder victims as the long-lost heir on the exact same day that the true connection between the victims had been discovered set off alarm bells deep within Violet's brain. It couldn't be a coincidence.

"It's got to be the motive," Benno said excitedly, though he'd said it many times already.

"This is the sheriff's department in Veil, Vermont," Derrick said into the phone. Sheriff Grogan had instructed him to contact the lawyer's office. "Hello, I need to speak to—yes, I'll hold."

Grogan leaned across the desk and told him, "Ask if Violet Hall was one of the people in line to inherit the fortune."

"This has got to be it," Benno repeated. "It's like you said—practically everyone around here is related. Someone has been systematically killing off the heirs to the fortune, down the line of inheritance, one at a time."

"For thirty years?" Cy said incredulously. "That's hella patience."

"And none of the heirs ever knew what was theirs," murmured Grogan. Her eyes were haunted. Cy and Violet approached her from either side. Cy put a hand on her mother's shoulder. Grogan said, "I remember hearing that Mrs. Hall, Violet's mother, died a year or two after her daughter. I thought, at the time, that she'd just lost the will to live. It never occurred to me..."

"But I don't understand," said Cy. "What good would it do anyone to just keep killing off the last victim's next of kin? The money would just keep going to random people."

"Because they didn't!" said Benno. "Sometimes the next of kin was killed *before* the heir, so that the money would pass on to someone else! Just think—some of these victims must have made wills, naming their own heirs. If the heir they chose died first, the money would go to their nearest relative instead. By targeting the victims in a specific order, the killer was able to control and manipulate the direction of the money. Here, I'll show you." He drew up a map of New York and New England across which a series of Xs marked towns where the killer had struck. "The woman we just heard about, who died in Frost, New York, she left everything she had to her fiancé. I know because the police suspected him, but he had an alibi, and, besides, her death couldn't be proved to be homicide. Then, three years later, her fiancé also died, but not before his brother met an untimely death. His brother *would* have inherited the fortune, but because the brother died first, the money ended up passing to the fiancé's next-closest relation: his grandparents. I'll bet you anything that when we finish tracing the relationships between the victims, we'll see a direct line of inheritance going all the way to Paul Hammond."

Urgency stirred in Violet as she realized where this was going. "So Hammond dies," she said, "and the fortune passes to his nephew, Matt Foley. Foley dies, and it goes to his cousin, Marcy, and then to her father." She looked at Benno. "Who was Byron Temple's next of kin?"

Benno hurriedly consulted his notes. "Well, if Sharon Brisbon was his aunt, then she would've been his closest relative."

"And she left everything she owned to Amy Chester," said Grogan, remembering.

"But Amy was already dead," pointed out Violet.

"So instead," Benno finished, "it all went to Kelly Upshaw."

Violet, Cy, Benno, and the sheriff all looked at each other. They spoke at the exact same time: *"Who's Kelly's next of kin?"*

"Oh, I know the answer to that," said a voice.

Chuck Benz stood in the doorway.

* * *

Fran helped Kristy strap the sleeping infant Rosie into her car seat. "All right," she grunted. "Everyone all set?"

Fastening her own seat belt, Kristy nodded but didn't say anything. She sniffled and swallowed thickly, a sign that her throat was too tight to speak.

From the front passenger seat came stony silence.

56

Fran made her way around and into the driver seat, took a deep breath, and let it out slowly. She gazed up through the windshield at the place that had been her family's home the past five years. "I'm gonna miss it," she said to herself.

A few seconds passed, and then Fran was surprised to notice Joy giving her a commiserating look. It was the first time Joy had acknowledged her existence all day. It made Fran feel a weight lift off her chest, though her heart was still heavy. It was all she could do to keep it from breaking as she started to back out of the driveway.

All of a sudden, four patrol cars screeched to a halt, surrounding her minivan. The three women looked all about in quickly growing alarm as the sheriff and several deputies got out and approached them, hands on holsters.

* * *

"Yes," said Fran, bemused, "Kelly Upshaw was my stepsister. We grew up together, more or less. In fact, I met Joy through her."

The sheriff and her deputies had escorted the Dosleys to the station. Joy and Fran now sat in the sheriff's office.

"Is Fran a suspect?" Joy demanded, showing signs of growing outrage.

Sheriff Grogan answered, "No," at the same time that Deputy Derrick answered, "Yes." Shooting him a hard glare, the sheriff said quickly, "I think it's much more likely that your familial tie to Ms. Upshaw puts you and your family in great danger."

"From the serial killer?"

"Exactly."

Fran grunted. "I think I'd prefer being a suspect."

"But why?" Joy pressed. "What does her past connection to Kelly have to do with it?"

Grogan chose her words carefully. "We believe Kelly Upshaw possessed something of great value, though she wasn't aware of it. We think whoever killed her intended for all her legal possessions to pass to someone else. In her will, she left everything to her niece, Amy Chester, but since Amy's dead, by default, the inheritance passes to her next closest relative."

Fran became pensive for a minute. "You think the killer knows exactly who would inherit, given the circumstances?"

"We think the killer is very careful and cognizant about all the legalities concerning inheritance," said Deputy Benno.

"Then you'd better dig back into Kelly's family ties, and fast," said Fran, "because I'm not her next of kin. Not legally."

The sheriff sat up straight. "What?!"

Joy, too, looked mystified, but then she gasped. "That's right! They disowned you!" To the sheriff she explained, "When she agreed to be my legal co-parent, Fran's family just up and made her an outcast!"

"That's when I changed my name to Dosley," Fran added.

Grogan was turning pale. "Then the next target could still be out there."

* * *

"Violet?"

Violet turned to see an elderly woman enter the station. Her hair was snow white and she was hunched over from age, but she moved quite spryly. Violet blinked in surprise. "Peggy? What are you doing here?"

Peggy Allen peered toward the sheriff's office. "Is Jen available?"

"She's escorting the Dosleys out of town. Deputy Derrick's the only one here."

Peggy wrinkled her nose at the mention of Derrick's name.

"Is there something I can help you with?"

Peggy let out an unsteady breath. There was sorrow in her eyes. "I asked them to let me be the one to tell her."

"Tell her what? Asked who?" Violet led the woman to a nearby bench.

"There are a number of firms working together to trace the line of inheritance from Torrance Lammwych," Peggy began. "I was consulted because I used to work for his solicitor. I was told the Veil sheriff wanted to know if Violet Hall was one of those through whom the inheritance passed."

Violet Grogan nodded.

"Torrance's son, Bobby, left everything he owned to his best friend, who, as it turns out, was Violet Hall's godfather. He lived in Oregon, though he had family here in Veil. They lived in a six-story apartment building."

Violet felt a shiver. "The one that burned."

"That's right. That's how they were killed. So when her godfather died a week later, Violet Hall was his only living heir."

"Jen said Violet was suspicious about that fire! That's why she was in the building the day she…"

Peggy glanced down. "I remember Jen, as a child, swearing black and blue that her friend had been murdered. And, just like everyone else, I didn't believe her." She looked into Violet's eyes. "After the firms called to consult me, I put two and two together. I know Sheriff Grogan will want to choose the right time to tell the townspeople the serial killer's true motive, but I just wanted to tell her…" She sighed.

Violet gave her a friendly pat on the arm. "I'll tell her," she promised.

After Peggy left, Cy promptly came out from behind the door

where she had been eavesdropping. "Wow," she said, "that's huge. I wonder how many other people will be big enough to admit Mom was telling the truth, and they were wrong."

Violet didn't answer. She was staring off after Peggy, and she was starting to frown.

"What's the matter? What are you thinking about?"

"Pressler."

A haunted look came over Cy. "What about him?"

"He mentioned Violet Hall when the killer confronted him."

"Right…"

"But *he didn't know about the inheritance.* He had no idea. Remember? He asked the killer specifically why they were doing it. So if he didn't know about the Lammwych fortune—"

"How could he have known that Violet Hall was a victim?" finished Cy.

Again, Violet replayed Pressler's conversation in her head. If only he'd mentioned a name, given some clue as to the identity of his murderer… But no, he'd chosen to spend the last moments of his life being morbidly jovial. *"I stumbled across your little homicide last year…"* Had he meant the murder of Paul Hammond, the semi driver? How frustrating it was that the one person who had happened to "stumble" upon the killer's identity was the one person who, rather than report it, would keep it secret in order to use the knowledge for his own profit.

Except he hadn't known the killer's identity back then. *"It never occurred to me that the killer I'd hired—was the killer!"* Something had happened between last year and now that had clued him in. The killer had probably intended to silence him all along but put it off as long as possible because it risked interfering with them reaching their goal, which apparently was a vast fortune.

"Whatever your goal is, you're close, but you're not there yet. And I'm not the only person who can stop you." Was that just brave talk, Violet wondered, or had Pressler really had faith in her? *"She's onto you, even if she doesn't know it yet. Sooner or later she'll piece it together, as I did."* But Violet didn't know the killer had taken someone's life last year! How could he expect her to piece it together without that key bit of knowledge?! It made no sense.

"Damn it, Pressler," Violet whispered. "Why didn't you just say the name?"

And then something occurred to her. Just before the killer confronted him, Pressler *had* said a name. He'd been muttering to himself. Violet had only been able to make out two words: "wall" and "Saul." Violet had already double-checked: there was no "Saul" living in Veil. Yet she couldn't help wondering…

Who was Saul?

* * *

"There." In the bullpen, Luther replaced the cap on the marker and stepped back from the dry-erase board so that Chuck could see the diagram clearly.

Chuck gave the mass of lines and scribbles a look of utter incomprehension. He pointed and said, "What is that?"

He was speaking of the diagram as a whole, but Luther seemed to think he was indicating the exact scribble his finger was pointing to. "That's you," he said.

Chuck stared blankly for a moment, then abandoning the effort to understand Luther's visual aid, he asked, "So am I an heir?"

Luther traced his finger in a zigzag pattern along the diagram from top to bottom. "You are…not!" He nodded with the satisfaction of having given the correct answer.

Chuck looked less than satisfied. "But you just said Matt

Foley was Paul Hammond's nephew, and he was an heir. I'm his nephew, too, just on a different side."

"Right, but, like, Matt was his great-nephew."

"I am, too!"

"No, you're his great-great-nephew."

"That's what I just said!"

"No, I mean, it's a different number of 'greats.'"

"What??"

"It's, it's a, um, it's a different number of, uh…" He moved his finger up and down on the board, but it failed to produce the right word. "Okay, look, Paul Hammond was the brother of Matt Foley's grand—" He squinted at a scribble near the top. "Grandparent, but for you, he was the brother of your *great*-grand…something. So it's a different—generation!" He pointed in triumph. "There are more generations!"

Deputy Derrick, on the phone nearby, glanced over in irritation.

"So I have more generations on my side than Foley's," said Chuck.

Luther nodded. "Yes!"

"So then I'm the heir!"

Luther nodded again. "No!"

Chuck threw up his hands with a scowl. "Well, if I'm not an heir, then why did the serial killer try to get me?!"

"Um…"

Derrick covered the phone's mouthpiece and snapped, "Because the killer was worried you might try and make a claim to the fortune, and wanted you out of the way, just in case. Hello?" he said into the phone. "Yes, I'm still here."

Luther jerked his head in Derrick's direction. "That's what I was gonna say."

Chuck still looked contentious, but Luther was saved from having to explain further by Cy and Violet entering the bullpen. Cy asked, "Chuck, do you know of *any* other relations Kelly had? Any who are still alive besides Fran Dosley?"

Chuck shrugged. "I only knew about Fran because I was put in charge of writing Kelly's obituary. Fran's the only one I found any record of."

"Was Kelly born in Veil?" asked Violet.

"No, she moved here to be near her niece, Amy."

"Yes," said Derrick into the phone, raising his voice slightly. "This is Deputy Derrick of the Veil Sheriff's Department."

"Maybe we should talk to someone from Kelly's hometown," suggested Cy.

Luther gestured at Derrick. "I think that's what he's doing."

"Yes, I'm very interested," said Derrick, poised to take notes. "Go ahead." He started writing. "I see. Uh-huh. Is he still alive? Oh. Well, that doesn't help us... A baby!"

Violet took an involuntary step forward.

"All right, thanks," said Derrick. "Yeah, let us know." He hung up and jotted down a few more notes.

"What'd they say?" asked Violet.

Derrick ignored her.

"Derrick, what did they say?!"

Derrick gave an exasperated sigh and with the air of, *if it'll shut you up,* he answered, "When Kelly Upshaw moved to Veil, she left behind a cousin."

"Right," said Chuck, "but he's dead now."

"He is," agreed Derrick, sounding very irritated, "thanks to a tornado nine years ago. But he and his wife left behind a baby girl. Kelly relinquished custody, so the baby was put up for adoption."

"What was the baby's name?" asked Cy.

"They don't know."

"Well, they have to find out! She could be the next target!"

"They're working on it! They know what's going on. This kid could be anywhere in the US. You need to stop telling everyone how to do their jobs."

"I'm not telling anyone anything, I'm just scared for that kid!"

"Are you trying to say I'm not?!"

"Hey," Luther stepped in between Cy and Derrick. "You should leave her alone."

Derrick stood up. "And maybe you should leave, period."

"Enough!" shouted Violet. She was trying to concentrate. The conversation had triggered a flash of memory, but she was having trouble seeing it clearly in her head. It was from Halloween night—the one date she *still* had trouble remembering since she had awakened in Veil. Something to do with Marcy. Something Marcy said…

"Blood-velvet cake," Violet murmured, then again, louder— "blood-velvet cake! Oh my god—*that's* what was nagging at me! How could the killer have known in the first place—?!" To Deputy Derrick she shouted, "It's Emma Thurmin! Emma Thurmin is the next target!"

"What are you *talking* about? You don't know that!"

Giving up on him, Violet turned to Cy. "Call your mom! Tell her it's Emma!" She started for the exit.

Cy said, "I'll go with you!"

"No! Stay here, where you're safe! Just tell her to hurry!"

As Violet ran out and Cy began dialing frantically on her phone, Derrick dismissed it all with a roll of his eyes. He sat back down to make another call, but the phone rang again before he could pick up the receiver. To his puzzlement, it was the same number he'd just been speaking to. He answered the phone. "Hello?"

* * *

Emma was busy packing her stuffed animals when she found herself beginning to cry. She loved her house and she didn't want to move out of it. Of course, their leaving wasn't supposed to be forever, but deep down, Emma couldn't help being afraid that she'd never see her home again.

She could hear her parents still arguing downstairs. She sat on her bed and cried silently for a few minutes. Then she went to the bathroom, blew her nose, and dried her eyes. She took the cup she used for brushing her teeth out of the medicine chest, filled it with water, and drank it.

As she headed back to her room, she noticed it was quiet downstairs. Had the argument finally stopped? "Mom?" she called softly. There was no answer. Clearing her throat, she tried again. "Mommy? Dad?"

Emma went downstairs.

Her mother she found sprawled on the living room floor by the sofa. No matter how hard Emma tugged at her or how loud she shouted, her mother wouldn't move. The same proved true of her father, splayed in the doorway between the dining room and the kitchen.

Emma needed help. She'd go next door and see if her neighbor was at home. If they weren't, she'd get her mother's cell phone. She was pretty sure she could remember the passcode.

That was her last thought before her legs suddenly felt wobbly and gave out beneath her, and she pitched forward into oblivion.

VI

I t was still afternoon, but the sky was fast approaching dusk.
Violet tried to match its speed as she raced through town,
across streets, through yards, over fences, taking every
shortcut she knew.

"You're gonna catch the killer?"

"Yes. I am."

"Before he gets anyone else?"

"I promise. We won't let him kill any more people."

Violet felt a deepening sense of dread, and she cursed her legs
for being so short.

*   *   *

The Thurmins' porch light shone in through the narrow
windows on either side of the front door. The eerie light cast
an orange rectangle on Emma's small, prone form.

A shadow fell on her as someone peeked inside.

*   *   *

Crossing the municipal building's parking lot seemed like a
good idea until Violet slipped on a patch of ice halfway across.
She scrambled to her feet but slipped again. "Aaaugh! No!!"
Standing gingerly, she moved with agonizing slowness across
the lot, which suddenly seemed completely paved with ice...

*   *   *

The front door was unlocked, as the Thurmins had been packing their car in the driveway. The uninvited visitor entered unseen and unheard.

Emma Thurmin's small body lay not very far inside the house. Her back rose and fell in a slow rhythm, accompanied by a light wheezing. A hand reached down, lightly brushed aside the blond hair that had fallen across her face and neck. A thumb peeled back Emma's left eyelid. The girl's body remained limp. She was completely unconscious.

From an inner coat pocket the visitor drew a long, sharp instrument. A few hours earlier, it had lain on Myrna Redpath's table, waiting to be sold. Once it had served its purpose, it would be buried where no one would ever find it.

The visitor brushed aside the few remaining strands of hair obscuring Emma's neck.

* * *

Violet felt the cold burning her lungs. She was not about to rest before making sure Emma was safe, but she hoped she'd be able to go back indoors soon. It must be thirty-something degrees Fahrenheit, and dropping.

Finally she could see the Thurmins' house up ahead. She sped up, remembering just in time to check the ground for icy patches. Zigzagging, she was just nearing the driveway when she heard a police siren behind her. Good—Jen had gotten here much faster than Violet had expected. Running here, herself, had probably been a waste of effort—

The patrol car swerved around Violet and halted just in front of her, between her and the house. To Violet's surprise, it was not the sheriff but a deputy who emerged from the car. "Derrick! What are you doing here? You're supposed to stay at the station! You can't just leave Cy all alone—"

"Shut up!" Derrick barked. "Shut up and don't move."

"Fine, I'll stay here." Violet backed away from the house. "Just hurry up and make sure Emma and her parents are okay—"

"I said, don't move!" Derrick hollered.

And he drew his gun and pointed it at Violet.

Violet might have forgotten to breathe had her lungs not been pounding so. She stared at Derrick with wide, incredulous eyes. "What—are you—*doing??!!*"

"I'm saving Emma Thurmin—*from you.*"

* * *

The intruder had a handful of Emma's hair and had pulled her head up and off the floor just far enough to reach around with the knife. The blade was almost touching the flesh of the girl's throat when a shout reverberated from outside. The intruder looked up and saw Violet and Deputy Derrick through a window.

The knife was withdrawn. Emma's head was lowered back to the ground.

Neither Violet nor any deputy was supposed to be here yet. If Emma's throat were slit now, Violet could prove her innocence by the total lack of blood on her clothes.

The intruder darted into the kitchen, then returned hastily with a roll of plastic wrap. It took only a few seconds to wrap a sufficient quantity around the child's head, fully covering her mouth and nose.

The task complete, the intruder made a quiet exit through the back door.

* * *

"Why did he leave?" Cy wondered aloud. "Mom told Derrick not to leave the station. What did he find out that was so important he had to go away?"

Luther didn't answer. He was frowning at his phone screen.

"What is it?"

Luther hurriedly pocketed his phone. "Uh, nothing."

Cy gave him a look.

"Something's happening at the Thurmin house," he admitted. "But I think you should stay here."

Cy had been about to check her own phone, but upon hearing this last comment, she grabbed her coat and replied, "I don't."

* * *

"Look, Derrick," said Violet tremulously, hands in the air, "I don't know what's going on, but Emma's in there, in danger—"

"Take one step and I'll shoot!" Derrick threatened, though Violet hadn't moved.

Violet looked about frantically. "Will you just stop and *think?!* Why haven't they come out?!"

"What??"

"We're out here yelling so loud, all the neighbors are coming out to see what's going on, so why aren't the Thurmins coming out, too?!"

Derrick could see the house next door out of the corner of his eye. Two people were watching from the porch. There were more behind him, but he kept his focus on Violet. "What did you do?"

"What did I—what??!"

"What did you do to the Thurmins?"

Violet shook her head in exasperation. "I haven't done anything! I just got here! You saw me!"

"No. You've been in the house already. Then you pretended to get here the same time I did. Emma's dead, isn't she."

"She might be if we don't go in and help!!" Violet gave him a pleading look.

"How did you 'figure out' Emma would be the next target?"

Violet let out a cry of despair and aggravation. Then, behind Derrick, she saw more patrol cars approaching. "Jen!" she hollered with a frantic wave.

Derrick roared, "Answer me!! How did you know?!"

"I, I—M-Marcy! Marcy told me, back in October, she told me Emma's adopted, and Emma's the right age!"

"That's it?"

"No!"

The patrol cars halted with a jerk in front of the house. Sheriff Grogan sprang out and advanced with her hand on her sidearm. "Deputy Derrick, what do you think you're doing?!"

Derrick didn't move or answer.

"Either lower that weapon or your badge is gone forever!"

Still he didn't respond. His eyes were fixed on Violet, who pointed desperately at the Thurmins' house. "Jen, something's wrong in there!!"

"Trent! Powell!"

The two deputies dashed obediently inside.

Grogan drew her weapon partway out of its holster. "Derrick…"

"I'm waiting for Violet to answer my question," said Derrick with frightening calm.

Violet spoke in a rush. "I'd been wondering why the killer left Kelly for Emma to find before dumping the body in our house, but in the back of my head I was wondering something else: how could the killer have known Emma would *find* the body? How did he know she was going out to the tree with the birds' nest every day? He must have been watching her! He was watching her because he was planning to kill her!"

"Sheriff!" Trent appeared at the front door. "I just called nine-one-one. Someone tried to smother Emma, left her with plastic wrap around her head."

"Oh my god!" Violet wailed.

"Powell's giving her CPR."

"What about the parents?" asked Grogan.

"They're both out cold. I think they've been drugged."

"Drugged…"

"Like the Dosleys!" Violet exclaimed.

"Check under the sink! Somebody might've tampered with their water system."

As Trent hastened to follow her orders, Grogan snapped at Derrick, "Deputy, this is your last warning!"

Dozens of pairs of eyes looked on in suspense to see what Derrick would do next. Still, he didn't move.

"Derrick, come on!" Benno hissed. "Violet isn't the serial killer!"

"I know she's not the serial killer. But she's *working* with the serial killer. And I know who it is."

"Who?"

Finally Derrick made a movement. He pivoted, directing his eyes and his weapon…

At Sheriff Grogan.

* * *

Every townsperson watching caught their breath.

Deputies Benno and Ziegler instantly drew their weapons and trained them on Deputy Derrick. Sheriff Grogan slowly moved her hand away from her own.

Violet was frozen, she was so stunned.

Benno started to speak, but Derrick beat him to it: "Magenta Grogan, as senior deputy, I'm relieving you of duty."

"The hell you are!" snarled Benno.

Derrick went on, "The police department in Kelly Upshaw's hometown called me back. Turns out they made a mistake. Kelly had another cousin, living in another town. *That* cousin is her next of kin."

Violet blinked in confusion. "But—Emma—"

"To Emma, he's an uncle. Like Kelly, he relinquished custody, but he's made a will leaving everything to her. So if she died before he did, everything he owns would go to his closest relative." Derrick twitched the gun at Jen Grogan. "You."

"What?" Grogan was clearly flummoxed.

Benno and Violet glanced at each other in shock.

"The killer was you all along," Derrick said through his teeth.

"No!" Benno protested. "That doesn't follow. She could be a future target."

"Oh, come on, Benno! Look at the pattern! The murders started here at almost the same time *she* moved back to Veil! One of the earliest victims, Violet Hall, was a girl *she* befriended— and she's admitted she was the last person to see her alive!"

Grogan trembled in outrage. "How dare you..."

"Jen was eleven!!" cried Violet.

Derrick threw her a contemptuous glance. "You think eleven-year-olds don't commit murder?"

"Stop it, Derrick!" snapped Benno. "You can't arrest her based on circumstantial evidence."

"You want evidence?" Derrick pointed at Violet with his free hand. "She's standing right there."

"What are you talking about?" asked Ziegler.

"Her amnesia's not real. Why do you think we haven't been able to find out who she is? Jen went and found someone already living off the grid, hired her to be an accomplice, promised her a cut of the fortune."

Grogan began, "You're inventing—"

"There were only two witnesses to this girl's first appearance! One was Grogan's daughter and the other one *was murdered that very night!*"

Violet risked a step forward. "Because *Pressler had him killed!* We heard him say so!"

"We? Who's we? We only have *your word.* Just like we only have your word that the killer broke into your house and left behind a burner phone, so he could call you and torment you, like something out of the movies!"

"Why would I make that up?!"

In a loud, firm voice Grogan said, "This has gone far enough. Ziegler, relieve Derrick of his sidearm."

But Ziegler didn't move. He was wearing a deep frown.

"Ziegler," Grogan repeated, urgency in her tone.

Ziegler gradually lowered his weapon. "I...want to hear the rest."

"What?!" Benno gawked at him.

In a firmer voice, Ziegler said, "I want to hear what else Derrick has to say!"

Violet turned to Grogan in growing despair, but the sheriff was too dumbfounded to notice.

"I could say a lot of things," drawled Derrick. "Like how strange it was that when these two women were kidnapped along with Trisha Sinclair, only Ms. Sinclair was kept unconscious. Everything that supposedly happened in that abandoned building is based on the word of the Grogans and no one else. Ms. Sinclair couldn't confirm or deny it."

Uncertainty flickered in Benno's eyes, then he blinked it away and pointed out, "They saved Chuck Benz!"

"Did they? Funny how the person they saved was the one and

only attempted victim whose death was *not* necessary to keep the fortune moving down the line of inheritance. I think they were surprised when sticking Mulroy's corpse in the car with Foley's didn't clear them of suspicion right away, so they staged an attempted murder just so they could prevent it."

"We almost *didn't* prevent it!" shouted Violet.

"Well, that's why you picked Chuck, in case you failed to save him. With him gone, you wouldn't have to worry about him making a claim to the fortune, however shaky."

"No! You're wrong!" Violet nearly shook with fury. "That booby-trap was set for Chuck on Halloween night! I remember hearing the killer whistle 'Pop Goes the Weasel'!"

"Really?" Derrick scoffed. "Funny that you and the killer crossed paths so many times that night."

"W-what??"

"That was the night Marcy Temple died—just hours after she spoke to you. She was killed in a playground, where *you were seen—all by yourself—around the time of her death.* In fact, she would've been found much earlier if it hadn't been for you stealing a golf cart!"

Ziegler gave a slow nod, with a dawning look on his face.

"Ziegler," said Grogan, half pleadingly, half admonishingly.

"It was also the night she led *you*"—Derrick pointed at Benno—"to evidence of what happened to *two other murder victims!*" He shook his head wonderingly. "Did you never stop and think, 'Oh—that's a coincidence'?!"

Benno made everyone flinch when his voice cracked out like a whip: *"Why would she lead me to the evidence when it's obvious the killer wanted to keep those murders a secret?! Why would they want us to know about a serial killer who's killing to inherit a fortune when it would point the finger right at them?!"*

74

For a moment Derrick said nothing, as if Benno's logic had stumped him. Then in a low voice, he said, "Are you *stupid*? No, of course you're not. So how can you not see it?! Benno...*we were never supposed to connect the serial killer with the Lammwych fortune!* Think of the number of people they knew they'd have to kill who lived in Veil! Of *course* someone would suspect foul play. They invented the serial killer to create a scapegoat, then they framed Kurt Riner!"

"That's a lie!" snarled Grogan.

"Why do you think only some of the victims were left with the 'Pop Goes the Weasel' signature and others weren't? They didn't want us to see the familial connection! *You* figured that out, yourself."

Benno frowned to himself, thinking hard. "That can't be right..."

"Ask yourself this: how is it we know about the Lammwych fortune in the first place?"

"Because the Lammwyches accused Violet—"

"Because Violet 'discovered' that the last will and testament of Torrance Lammwych didn't actually exist. It's thanks to her that after all these years, the money is no longer in limbo—*just in time for the Grogans to inherit it.*"

Very slowly, Benno's eyes turned from Derrick to stare at Grogan and Violet. There was something in them that hadn't been there before.

Violet felt a chill. "Benno...?"

* * *

Cy was nearly out of breath by the time she and Luther came within view of the Thurmins' home. Catching sight of the scene up ahead, she skidded to a stop. "What the—?!"

Deputy Derrick had his gun trained on Cy's mother, while

Violet looked on in fright. Deputies Benno and Ziegler also had their guns drawn; Benno's was trained on Derrick while Ziegler's was pointed at the ground. Benno started to lower his weapon as well.

Cy drew breath to call her mother, but all at once Luther grabbed her and pulled her behind a pickup truck parked on the side of the street. "Wait!" he whispered. "We don't know what's happening."

Peeking out, they saw Deputy Trent come out of the house. They were too far away to hear what he was saying. He looked agitated. Cy was tempted to ask one of the neighbors what was going on. There were dozens of them standing in their yards, watching, some recording on their phones.

Suddenly Cy's mother shouted at Trent, and her words were clear: "You and Powell focus on saving Emma! That's an order!"

"Wait a minute!" exclaimed Violet as Trent went back inside. "That's it! Jen and I were here alone with the Thurmins just this morning! If we wanted to attack them, why didn't we do it then?!"

"Because that wasn't your plan!" Derrick shot back. "You couldn't risk Emma running away while you took down the parents. You used Kelly Upshaw's body to get the family out of the house so you could tamper with the water system. You must've saved the contraption that was used on *your* house back in November."

"Check my vehicle!" bellowed the sheriff. "You won't find any trace of Kelly's body!"

"You could've wrapped it in plastic!"

"How could I have moved her on my own?!"

"Your daughter could've helped you!"

Cy gasped.

"She couldn't have, she was with the Dosleys!"

"And where are the Dosleys?"

"What do you mean, where—? We just escorted them out of town to a secure location!"

Derrick wheeled on Violet. "And where were you?"

"Before the funeral, I was with Candy!"

"Doing what?"

"We—we were sleeping together, you prick! But she can vouch for me!"

"Really? Then where is Candy now?"

"She—well, she's gone. I asked her to leave town, for her safety."

"How convenient. The Dosleys are incommunicado, and you asked your alibi to leave town." He turned back to the sheriff. "Just like you made your husband leave—maybe to get him out of your way, or maybe so you wouldn't have to share the inheritance with him."

Jen's eyes were deadly. "Are you done?" she growled.

The squeal of a siren made all of them twitch. The ambulance was approaching, red and white lights flashing.

Derrick glanced at the lights, then he thundered, *"Don't move!!"* (Though, as before, neither Violet nor the sheriff *had* moved.) "Get on the ground! Right now! Face-down!"

Frightened, Violet glanced at Benno and Ziegler, but neither gave any sign that they were going to intercede.

"Violet," Jen said calmly, "it's okay, just do what he says. It'll be all right."

"Shut up! I said, on the ground!"

Violet and Jen Grogan each went down to one knee.

Jen started to move her other leg—when suddenly she gasped.

Something had caught her eye.

Cy stared back at her from down the street, hand over her mouth, eyes wide with terror.

Derrick turned to see what Jen was looking at. "Hey!!"

He started to aim his gun in Cy's direction.

"NO!!!"

Jen ran at him full-tilt.

VII

BANG!

All the onlookers ducked, dropped, or screamed when the shot rang out.

With a shriek, Violet dove for cover, leaving Benno and Ziegler to try to intervene in the mad, writhing scuffle between Derrick and Grogan. The sheriff had hold of the deputy's wrist and was determined to wrest away the gun, clearly content to batter him in the process.

"Mom!!" hollered Cy.

She started forward, but Luther grabbed her and jerked her back. "No! That guy's crazy! Come on! Come *on*, we gotta run!"

Cy glanced back at her mother once before following him.

The two combatants twirled in place, jabbing, kneeing, wrenching, struggling to stay upright. Derrick roared in agony as Grogan head-butted him.

Ziegler waited for what he thought was the right moment and then darted in—only for the wrestlers to suddenly twist about, whipping the gun in Derrick's outstretched hand SMACK into the unlucky deputy's skull. Ziegler dropped to the ground, out cold.

What also dropped was the pistol.

Derrick made a beeline for it, but Grogan caught him from behind, quickly putting him in an arm lock. Holding him as a shield between her and Benno, the sheriff threw back her head and hollered, "Run!! *Ruuuuuuun!!!*"

She didn't know that Cy had already fled.

Thinking the directive was intended for her, Violet obeyed.

Derrick yelped in pain as Grogan countered his attempts to break free of the arm lock.

Benno made jerky forward movements, his face a mask of turmoil. "Just stop!" he pleaded, though it wasn't clear to whom he was speaking.

All at once Derrick seemed to remember there was another gun within his reach. His free hand went to Grogan's holster.

"No!" cried Benno, and, knowing how risky it was, he darted forward.

Derrick drew the sheriff's gun, but before he could do anything with it, Grogan spun him round. Her movements were so fast, they were almost a blur. Within moments, Derrick was disarmed, pummeled, and sent flying to the ground in an undignified heap. Next moment, Benno reached them—

And instantly Grogan aimed the gun and clicked the safety.

Perhaps the movement was instinctual, or perhaps it was a strategy she hadn't fully thought through. Whatever the case, Veil's sheriff was now pointing a loaded gun at the town's most beloved deputy.

It was impossible to tell which of them was the more shocked.

At some point during the melee, Deputies Trent and Powell had come out of the house. Trent now came down the porch steps—

"Stop!" shouted Grogan, pointing the gun in his direction. Watching the three conscious deputies carefully, she sidestepped, found Derrick's dropped weapon with her foot, and picked it up. She knew the entire village was watching her, the sheriff, threaten her own deputies with loaded firearms.

She would deal with that after she was sure her daughter was safe.

She backed away until the bulk of the parked ambulance was between her and the armed men. She saw Benno's eyes before he was lost from view. She'd seen him look at her like that once before, and it broke her heart all over again.

She turned and sprinted down the street, in the direction she thought Cy had run. Behind her, she heard Derrick waking up and yapping out commands.

The hunt had begun.

* * *

What is happening??

The moment she had the thought, Violet was nearly overwhelmed with panic. For she had had that thought before, at almost exactly this spot. It had happened four months ago, when Violet was blundering through the trees and bushes without the slightest idea who she was or why she was here, or where here was.

For one heart-stopping moment, Violet considered the possibility that it was still that day, that she was still blundering, that she'd only imagined the past four months and everything she'd done, everyone she had met and loved. That she would never, ever make it out of this forest…

She tripped and fell face-first into the snow. The wet and cold shocked her back to her senses.

When Jen had shouted at her to flee, Violet had considered running behind the house and into the trees and hiding there. However, her deathly fear of getting lost in the woods—

especially in the dark, as it would be soon—steered her down another street. There she found a bend in the road with a copse of trees bordering closely. Here she charged into the woods without hesitation: this was the spot where she, Jen, and Cy had emerged into Veil with the girl Megan Toombs, after having rescued her. Violet knew this part of the woods and could navigate them—so long as she kept to the route she'd taken before.

The snow blanketing every surface made recognition more difficult, but thanks to her memory she soon came across the spot where she'd collapsed for a while, where Emma had found her—

Emma—someone had wrapped *plastic* around her head!!!

White-hot anger made her stop in her tracks. What was she running for? She had to go back and solve the mystery, and stop this serial killer once and for all! They were so close, she could just feel it! If the killer really hadn't meant for them to connect the murders to the Lammwych inheritance, as Derrick had said, then—

Derrick.

Aggravation poured onto her anger. They already had enough problems without him adding on his ego-fueled paranoia.

Then again—the thought whispered from the back of Violet's mind—even without him, as soon as it came to light that the Grogans potentially stood to inherit, someone was *bound* to suspect them. And even though Derrick had his biases, the sheer amount of circumstantial evidence against the Grogans would've given anyone pause, investigator or no.

Was it possible...

Had the serial killer been playing an even *longer* game than they'd thought? Drugging Trisha, staging the discovery of

Kelly's body, killing Marcy in the playground, maybe even somehow inducing the Lammwych family to prosecute Violet—had it all been a far-reaching strategy to frame Jen, Cy...and herself?

But what about the money? Apparently it now belonged to this mysterious relative of Jen's, but if he were the culprit, he wouldn't have any motive for murdering Emma.

Would he?

"I made a promise..."

The killer felt they owed someone something. That didn't sound like someone who simply wanted to collect a reward for their efforts. Gaining the money was not the point, at least not by itself. There had to be more to it. But what?

Unless the mysterious relative was a secret resident of Veil, Violet was sure the killer wasn't he. The killer was *here*. It was someone she'd met.

Who???

Violet heard a twig snap behind her, and she sped off.

As long as Deputy Derrick was in charge of local law enforcement, it was too dangerous to be out in the open. She'd stay hidden until Jen got things back under control.

Violet was sure it wouldn't take her too long.

* * *

What have I done??

Jen Grogan, dashing through the streets of Veil, knew she had just made a mess. No, she told herself, that wasn't fair. The mess hadn't been her fault at all, she'd just...made it messier.

Why did I leave Cy alone with Deputy Derrick in the first place?! I should've known I couldn't trust him to look after her! Now Cy was alone with Luther Hennessey, whom Jen doubted would last long in a fight, against a deputy or the serial killer. And now that Jen knew she and her daughters were all potential targets…

Jen whipped out her phone as she doubled back, and started to dial. Cy and Luther weren't on any of the streets that led downtown. Perhaps to the school?

Jen was sprinting so fast she nearly keeled over when she came to a dead stop. Lightning-quick, she flattened herself behind a parked snow plow, and waited for the patrol car to pass by. They were combing the streets for her. *How am I ever going to fix this??* She had crippled her deputies' trust in her with deception, and now she'd lost it altogether.

Jen would find a way to undo the damage. She *must*.

But her children came first.

Having stopped, it was easier to put her phone to her ear and listen to the phone on the other end. It was ringing…then it went to voicemail. "Azura—" That was as far as Jen got before the connection died. It had happened many times since Azura had gone to Antarctica for her internship.

Cursing, Jen checked for the patrol car. Seeing it had passed, she dashed to the next intersection. There was still no sign of Cy or Luther. Where could they have gone? What else was close by?

Luther's house! Jen had memorized the address as soon as Cy started dating him in December.

Sure enough, when Jen backtracked and turned a corner, she saw Luther's pickup truck pulling out of the driveway.

"*Cy!!*"

She dashed after it, but it was no use. The truck was already a block away.

Without hesitation, Jen darted to the nearest parked car and smashed the window. It took her just under a minute to silence the alarm and hot-wire the car. As she pulled away in the direction the pickup had gone, she dialed Azura again and waited for the phone on the other end to finish ringing.

Nothing bad was going to happen to her girls tonight.

* * *

"Quick, this way!" hissed Luther.

"What?" Cy glanced in confusion down the cross-street. "I thought we were going to your house!"

"No, they'd look there! They saw me with you!" Luther took her hand, and she ran with him.

They bounded down Settler Street, which ran downhill toward the river. Cy glanced back and glimpsed uniformed figures racing after them.

Deputies. Her mother's *deputies* were chasing her. How could this be happening??

At the bottom of the hill, they sped along Riverbank Road till they came to the footbridge across Greene River. Breathless, Luther asked, "How well do you know the, the…" He gestured to the woods on the far side of the river.

"I know the trails," Cy wheezed, and together they hared across the bridge.

At the far end, Luther ducked down behind the bridge-frame and said, "You go on ahead. Take the ravine trail."

"What? Why?"

"If they start across the bridge, I'll let them see me and lead them along the other trail."

Cy stared at him.

"Go!" Luther urged her.

Cy knelt in front of him, reached out and stroked the side of his face.

It seemed to take Luther a moment to realize she wanted him

85

to kiss her, and he did so. It was a brief kiss, as if he was unsure whether this was really all right. Cy pulled him back, and the next kiss was longer, wetter. When they pulled away, both their faces were bright red, and not just from exertion.

"Hey," said Luther, "do you wanna—I mean, after all this stuff is, like, over, do you wanna—"

"Ask me later." Cy gave him a peck on the cheek and ran off down the ravine trail.

* * *

At the last moment, Violet remembered to halt before plunging through the trees into the Greene River rapids. She'd been carried downstream in this river once before, and once was enough. She followed alongside the river, squeezing between the trees and bushes—a task made slightly easier than last time by winter's defoliation. She could still hear noises behind her that might have been a deputy in pursuit, but the forest was too thick for her to see.

Being swept downriver might have nearly drowned her, but it certainly had taken less time. It felt like ages before Violet finally broke free of the thicket and found herself in another familiar location: Riverbend Park. A wide-open space with a volleyball court, a small pavilion, and several picnic tables along the riverbank. Just over the hill, the top of a batting cage was visible. Beyond the baseball diamond, she knew, was a hockey pavilion.

On the day she'd been struggling not to drown in the river, Violet had caught at a thick root protruding from the bank and used it to haul herself out. It was the first thing she'd managed to grab after flailing at several branches overhead that were far out of her reach. A piece of luck, that root, followed quickly by another: meeting Cy. And Rob Mulroy.

And just that night, Rob was killed. Deputy Derrick was right, the coincidence was striking.

But what if it really was just that, a coincidence? What if the serial killer had taken Pressler's commission and waited for the right time to use it to implicate the Grogans? That *had* to be it. No one could've predicted Violet showing up and forming a bond with Cy and Jen.

Could they? Could someone possibly have predicted Violet would appear in Riverbend Park at an exact time?

"Don't move or I'll shoot!"

Apparently someone had just done exactly that.

* * *

Where is he taking her??

Jen had followed Luther's pickup truck out to County Route 127. Perhaps he was taking Cy to wherever his parents had evacuated to. Well, Jen appreciated his initiative, but it wasn't good enough for her. She was going to get them to pull over, then she was going to drive them both to the county seat, where she would contact the state police and have them take charge of the case. If she and her daughter had to be kept in custody for a short while, at least it wouldn't be James Derrick's custody.

Except that she seemed to have lost the pickup.

Had it turned off somewhere? Jen didn't think there were any crossroads this close to the outskirts of town, but she was sure it had only been a few seconds—half a minute at most—from the time the truck turned onto Route 127 before she followed it. She should be able to see the truck just up ahead. Was Luther driving with the headlights off?

Jen was reaching for her cell phone to call Cy when red and blue lights blared to life behind her.

For a second, she hesitated. A deep instinct told her to catch up to her daughter before all else, damn the consequences. But now that she'd been spotted, the longer she prolonged the pursuit, the more danger she'd put Cy in once she reached her. And she wasn't even sure she was on the right track anymore. Perhaps that wasn't Luther's truck she'd been following after all.

But where did it go??

The patrol car's sirens squawked, and she pulled over. In an instant, she had her phone to her ear and waited for Cy to answer. By the time it went to voicemail, whoever had pulled her over was tramping toward her door. "Cy," she said quickly, "wherever you are, stay there. Once I sort this out, I'll come find you. Everything's gonna be all right."

A hand rapped on her window.

"I love you."

Jen hung up the phone and rolled down the window.

She felt a swell of relief when she saw who it was. "Benno—"

"I need you to hand me the guns one at a time," Benno said shortly.

Jen complied.

"Now step out."

Jen got out of the car. "Benno, I need you to contact the state police. We can't let Derrick stay in charge of the department. This has gotten *way* out of hand."

Benno's face was absolutely devoid of expression, though his eyes bore a trace of…something she couldn't identify. "Are you carrying any other weapons?"

Jen tilted her head appealingly. She tried not to sound too desperate. "Benno…"

Benno held out his hand.

One after another, Jen gave up her taser, club, and two knives.

"Don't move, please." Benno deposited the weapons in his patrol car, then came back. Jen had not moved. He stood before her a moment, as if fortifying his resolve.

That's what she'd seen in his eyes. Resolve.

"Benno, I'm sorry."

Her words came in a rush. Benno blinked, caught off-guard.

"Back at the Thurmins', things happened so fast, I didn't mean to draw on you. I was scared for Cyanne."

Benno said nothing, but it was clear she had his attention.

"And I've been trying to find the right time—and the courage—to tell you… I've been thinking about what you said to me. What you said the night Pressler died. I'm still on the fence about some of it, but…maybe you were right. Maybe you were right about everything. That's why I wanted to talk, to have another chance to listen. Maybe if I'd listened before…maybe if I'd known better, I wouldn't have alienated all the other deputies, and it wouldn't have been so easy for Derrick to…"

Benno's expression hadn't changed an iota.

"I'm not saying this to try and manipulate you. I'm saying it because, depending on what you do next, it might be my last chance. I should've listened to you, and I'm sorry I let you down. You and everyone else." She took a deep breath and let it out. "I trust you. Whatever you do next, I know it'll be the right thing."

She looked at him steadily and waited.

She didn't have to wait for long.

"Magenta Grogan, I'm arresting you on suspicion of multiple homicide. You have the right to remain silent…"

* * *

Disregarding the command given by the voice, Violet dashed back into the woods.

BANG!

A bullet whizzed close by her head. Violet flattened herself to the ground. It was dark enough that her pursuer couldn't see her in the trees, but if she ran, he might track the movement.

"Come out of there!" snapped Deputy Derrick. "You can't get away, and I will use deadly force if you try!"

Violet's mind raced. Could she evade him by crawling? That would only work if it were just him, without any backup. But even then—

Suddenly it occurred to her: where *was* his backup?

"If you're waiting for ex–Sheriff Grogan to come bail you out, don't bother! Benno picked her up in a stolen vehicle, trying to skip town, and Cyanne was just spotted on the Greene River footbridge. You're all only making it worse the longer you run."

Violet decided to risk a response. "Where are the other deputies?"

"They'll be along. Now come out of there."

Was he lying? Were they already out there, waiting to ambush her? "When the other deputies get here, I'll come out."

"You'll come out of there *now*, because I'm telling you to!"

"I don't think so."

"You don't think I'll really shoot you, but I will!!"

I believe you, thought Violet. *That's why I'm not coming out.*

She took a deep breath to find some calm. She kept talking to stall for time, but in her mind's eye, drawing from her memory, she gave daylight to the park and made the thicket of trees translucent.

"How are you going to justify shooting an unarmed suspect, Deputy? You could get in a lot of trouble."

"At least you wouldn't be able to kill anyone else!"

In her head, she floated out of the thicket and across the sunlit park, searching for something, *anything* that might save her. "Even if you really believed that," she said aloud, "that's not why you're going to shoot me, is it."

"What are you talking about?"

Finding nothing of use in the park, she tried the river.

"It took me six minutes and twelve seconds to run from the sheriff's station to the Thurmins' house. All those things you said, all that circumstantial evidence—you couldn't have thought of all that in six minutes. You've been thinking about this a long time, planning how you'd set us up."

"Set you up?! Are you kidding?! What about how you set up the sheriff?!"

"No one set up Dubowski. He was a rapist and a murderer."

"He protected this town! If he decided someone had to be sacrificed for its safety, that was his prerogative! The town owed him tribute!"

"Trib—?! Is that what you think Bethany was?! What he did to her—"

"She's *nothing!!* Have you *met* her?? She might've finally been worth something if she'd given the sheriff some pleasure!"

"You're deranged."

"I'm *loyal!!* Even when I vouched for the Grogans, I was being loyal! I knew the sheriff would have to dismiss them as suspects for lack of evidence, but if they turned out to be guilty, he'd be held accountable for letting them go! I vouched for them so *I'd* be the one to take the heat!"

Violet opened her eyes. She'd located a possible escape, but there was still a risk.

She'd have to play him very carefully.

"If you were really loyal," she said, "why didn't you swear to avenge his death?"

"What makes you think I didn't?"

Violet got slowly to her feet. "When I woke up from my coma, you were in my hospital room. You were going to kill me, weren't you. If it hadn't been for Deputy Hayden..."

Breathily Derrick said, "You were never meant to be part of this town. If it weren't for you, Pressler would never have become mayor, and the sheriff..." His voice took on a sobbing quality. "We left you alone for too long, and look what you did." Then, apparently getting control of himself, his voice became hard. "Time to come out of there."

Violet pivoted, faced a certain direction. "Aren't you forgetting something?"

There was a *click* as Derrick released the safety catch on his weapon. "What's that?"

Violet bent her knee in a runner's crouch. "If your intention is murder...you can't afford to shoot me in the back!"

And she shot off through the trees.

For a dreadful moment she wondered: would Derrick simply shoot her, to show her she miscalculated? Or would her plan work—would he chase after her, to prove to her he didn't have to shoot her to take her down?

A savage roar and the crashing of branches gave her her answer.

Derrick felt the trees slashing at his hands as he shielded his face, but he could just see the running figure ahead of him. She wasn't getting away. Not this time. Already he'd guessed her strategy. She was trying to lead him toward the river. All of a sudden, she'd dodge to the side, and he'd trip and fall into the rapids. Well, it wouldn't work. He was already closing in. Another few steps and he'd be able to reach out and grab her...

He took another step and found that the ground had disappeared.

Violet heard him cursing and blubbering downstream as she hung from the tree branch that extended over the river. Being a short person, she hadn't been sure she could jump high enough to reach it.

Would anyone believe her if she tried to tell them what Derrick had just admitted to? Anyone apart from Cy and Jen?

Violet's hands started to slip. The first thing she had to worry about now was getting down onto solid ground.

* * *

Cy wished Luther had come with her. She could barely see her surroundings, and apparently somewhere along the trail she'd lost her phone, so she couldn't light her way. Twice now she'd thought she heard a deputy approaching, creeping up on her. That or an animal—a bear, perhaps. How long would she have to hide out here? Maybe she could find somewhere else to hide, somewhere other than these creepy woods. Where else could she go? Was there someone who would help her hide? Myrna? Delphine and Althea? Em or Neesha? There were several possibilities, but Cy would never be able to try any of them if she didn't make it back into the town proper. She turned around to head back along the trail.

Apparently, she turned too fast. It suddenly felt as if the world was spinning. She stumbled. She was so dizzy, she thought for a moment that she felt someone actually push her. She fell, and instinctively she reached out and grabbed at a rock to steady herself.

Instantly, she sensed something was wrong. As she lay there, clutching the rock sticking out of the ground, she took a deep breath and blinked several times. Finally her head began to clear.

She shrieked.

She was not lying on the ground.

She was hanging over the edge of a cliff.

If it had been daylight, and if she had cared, Cy might have noted the coincidence that this was just about the same spot where she had come close to falling into the ravine last October, on the day she met Violet.

"HELLLLLP!!!"

She tried to pull herself up over the edge. Her feet found no toehold. It felt as if moving her fingers even an inch would disrupt her grip completely.

"Somebody helllp!!"

She didn't care if the deputies caught her now. Better to be put in jail than to—

A footstep crunched in the snow.

"Over here! I'm over here! Quick, help me!"

The footsteps approached slowly.

"Hurry! Please!"

A silhouette appeared above her.

"Please! I'm gonna fall!!"

The silhouette didn't move. Whoever it was knelt at the edge of the ravine, staring down at her.

Cy suddenly had an awful feeling...

Then a light switched on. Cy blinked, then gasped. "Oh, thank God! Luther! Hurry, get me up!"

Luther's face was neutral in the light shining from the phone in his hand.

It took Cy a moment to realize...*the phone was hers.*

"Luther...?"

Luther opened his mouth. *"All around the cobbler's bench..."*

Cy's heart turned to ice.

"The monkey chased the weasel—"

"NNOOOOOOOOOO!!!!"

"The monkey thought 'twas all in fun—"

"Help me! *Hellllp!!!* He's gonna kill me!!!"

"Pop! goes the weasel."

Through her fear Cy tried to think clearly. Anything she could possibly do to stall him, anything… "What did you promise??"

"I've—" Luther stopped.

"Tell me—what was your promise? What was it? Why is it so important?"

He gazed down at her as if considering.

Just get him monologuing, thought Cy. *Someone's got to be searching these woods by now. They'll see the light from the phone, they'll come and…*

Luther was smiling. *"I've no time to wait and sigh…"*

"NO!!"

"I've no time to tease-l…"

"Please!!"

Luther tossed the phone over Cy's head, into the ravine. It shattered below. *"Kiss me quick… I'm off…"* He whispered: "Goodbye."

"Mom—!!"

VIII

J en was silent in the back of the patrol car, her wrists
chained together. There was nothing left to say.

She'd driven the stolen car far enough out of town that
the quickest way back was the junction with Route 24, which
in Veil turned into Riverbank Road. Deputy Benno was taking
the shortest route to the sheriff's station, and the jail cells.

Benno frowned as, up ahead, what appeared to be a light show
came into view.

Jen caught sight of it and craned her neck to get a better look.

The light was from a fire truck. It was one of several
emergency vehicles parked at the opening of the Greene River
footbridge. As Benno slowed to a stop, they could see more
lights at the far end of the bridge. Many of them were moving.

Benno thumbed on his radio. "Benno to all deputies: there
appears to be some kind of activity at the footbridge. Can
someone tell me what's going on?" His query was met with
silence.

After a moment's hesitation, Benno turned off the engine, got
out of the car, and headed across the footbridge, leaving Jen
secured in the back.

Except that Jen knew these patrol cars from hood to taillight, and even in handcuffs she knew how to exploit each one's weakness.

Along the ravine trail Benno found a conglomeration of deputies, paramedics, and rescue workers. When they gave him their news, he had to steady himself against a tree. Only fragments of further explanations made it through his ears to his conscious brain: "Heard her scream when they were searching...kept it out of radio chatter...might cause your prisoner to become unstable...chances are slim..."

Benno had to force air into his lungs to keep breathing.

When Jen Grogan walked past him, he almost didn't notice. In fact, at first, neither did any of the other deputies, her manner was so natural, as if she more than anyone else was supposed to be there.

It was less for the purpose of restraining her and more to save her from a painful sight that, as Jen approached the edge of the ravine, Benno launched himself at her. By that point Derrick, too (still soaking wet and pretending not to be shivering), had noticed her and raised the alarm.

Jen Grogan looked over the edge.

Her daughter Cyanne lay below, she couldn't tell how far down. Dancing lights played about her, cast by the people trying to get her out. The lights were moving, but Cy was not.

"CYYYYYYYYYY!!!!"

Peripherally Jen was aware of something pulling her back. She wouldn't have cared except that it was causing her to lose sight of her little girl.

"Nooo!! Cyyyyy!!!"

Gradually it registered that multiple men were trying to restrain her. What were they thinking? Didn't they realize that her daughter needed her? That Jen had to be with her?

How could they not see that? She tried to tell them.

It came out as her screaming her daughter's name a third time.

When that didn't work, she tried telling them a different way.

The deputies had seen Jen fighting earlier, and so they thought they knew what they were dealing with. What they didn't realize—and what they now discovered—was that Jen had been holding back.

One after another, the deputies hit the ground before they knew what was happening. Even handcuffed, Jen took them out like they were nothing. Each brief moment she broke free, she darted back to the cliff edge to shout her daughter's name, as if by shouting loud enough, she could make Cy wake up.

None of the deputies had yet been knocked out this time, but it was clear they were fighting a losing battle—even though it was equally clear that Jen Grogan had no interest in escaping. Nevertheless, Deputy Derrick all at once decided he had had enough. "Stand clear!" he shouted.

He drew his sidearm.

The other deputies froze, alarm and indecision written on their faces.

Jen was back at the ravine, shouting desperately downward.

Derrick aimed the weapon and clicked the safety.

Jen reached toward Cy with a mournful wail.

Just before Derrick could pull the trigger, someone else did.

Jen went rigid. She shook, convulsing as the taser sent electric shocks through her body. She might have plummeted into the ravine if Ziegler hadn't been quick with his club, and guided her fall.

Benno dropped the taser and set about transporting his prisoner to a jail cell.

Violet, watching from several meters away, sank down behind a large tree, curled into a ball, and sobbed as quietly as she could.

* * *

Luther dialed a certain number. "It's done. Good thing you decoyed the sheriff with my truck. I'll meet up with Kurt and check in later." He smirked. "I got her to kiss me, you know. Like in the song. Made it easier to get her phone without her noticing... Yeah, all right, I will." He hung up.

* * *

Violet sat at the river's edge a mile from where Cy had fallen. Her knees were drawn up to her chin. She no longer shivered. Her bones felt as numb as her heart.

As if to underscore this, Violet thought to herself distantly that it should be raining, storming. Such weather would be appropriate for all that had just happened.

Jen was in jail. The town believed she was the serial killer. Violet was a fugitive. And Cy...

The spot where Violet was sitting was part of the second trail that branched off from the footbridge. Nearby was a trail marker with an LED light. Violet could see her dim, bluish reflection in the water. The last time she had felt this lost, Cy had helped her. The girl had wanted nothing in return. She was just kind. She'd given Violet a name, a home, a feeling of hope. In a sense, she'd even given Violet a face. The first night of Violet's new life, she'd discovered she had no idea what she looked like. Cy had brought her to a mirror and—

Thunder rumbled in the distance. The rain Violet had decreed was approaching. But she didn't notice. She had half-risen, staring fixedly at her reflection.

"Mirror..." She had spoken that word several times while in a coma. Candy had said so.

"She's onto you," Pressler had told the serial killer, talking of Violet, *"even if she doesn't know it yet. Sooner or later, she'll piece it together, as I did."*

Mirror...

Violet got unsteadily to her feet, still staring at herself. "Mirror, mirror...on the *wall*...who's the fairest...of us all!" Not Saul!

She turned in place. Her breath came fast. "Mirror, mirror, on the wall... Mirror, mirror, on the wall..."

She was close. So close. The answer was like a forgotten word on the tip of her tongue. She could remember everything else—she would remember this, too!

"Mirror," she repeated, her voice growing higher in pitch, "mirror...mirror...*mirror—*"

She went still.

Then, slowly, everything about her relaxed. Her voice dropped, became husky: "Mirror." She let out a soft sigh.

She knew who the serial killer was.

TO BE CONTINUED...

WINTER IN VEIL

A Mystery Novella Series
by Miles Ledoux

#1 VIOLET
#2 GOOD WITCH, BAD WITCH
#3 JOHNSON'S WELDER
#4 RING AROUND THE ROSIE
#5 POP GOES THE WEASEL
#6 APRIL
#7 OVERKILL
#8 THE THIRD WILL
#9 SALT & VINEGAR
#10 MEMORY LANE
#11 THE IMPOSTOR
#12 KISS ME QUICK
#13 BEHIND THE DARKNESS

About the Author

Miles Ledoux was born in upstate New York and started writing murder mysteries at the age of nine. His first paid writing gig was in 2007, when a local theatre chose one of his plays for their summer melodrama. He received other royalties after moving to Los Angeles for graduate school, where he wrote, directed, and produced several mystery dessert theatre plays. He also started a side business designing and running mystery party games while working as a martial arts instructor.

Currently the author resides in Springfield, Vermont. Despite having lived in five different states, he has remained active in community theatre as a playwright, director, and actor. He also has a YouTube channel where he compares Agatha Christie adaptations to the books they were based on. His handle is @MysteryMiles.

Miles loves books, cats, music, Star Trek, Peanuts, and owns an ever-growing number of variations of the board game Clue. His favorite author is Lloyd Alexander.

You can connect with me on:

🌐 https://www.ledouxmysteries.com